Child of Fate

Book One of the Ka'Zi Trilogy

E. Renee Sobien

THE WEST - ABOVE THE RING

ARCTIC TERRITORIES

DOROV OCEAN

Beriniat Steppes

Loriar Range

Beriniat River

Crystal Lake

LORIAR

Great Beriniat Forest

★ BERINIAT

KAI'NDE OCEAN

Mt. Terin

Markat Range

Loriar Swamp

Loriar Desert

MARKAT

Taniar River

Taniar Volcanic Range

Loris River

TANIAR

TANIM ✦

DONIER

PAREM CITY

Lake Parem

Parem Desert

Kori Lake

Taniar Bay

Taniar Archipelago

PAREM

Great Savanna

LOSOR OCEAN

Parem Jungle

THE WEST - BELOW THE RING

N
W · E
S

Parem Jungle
DOREN
ARLEMO
PARMOS

THE ISLAND

DOROV OCEAN

Great Parem River

DAKOR CITY

Parem Plains

Liar Canyon

PAREM

Great Dakor Forest

DELAR

Dakor Bay

Mt. Korus

KORUS

Dakor Lake

DAKORIS

Lior River

Great Southern Range

LOSOR OCEAN

Dakoris Glaciers

Frost Island

GREAT SOUTHERN ICE MASS

Prologue

A woman leaned against a dingy stone wall in an alleyway, swaying weakly. Bloodstains dotted her gray cloak, and the pink scarf around her head stuck to her skin with sweat. Leaning against her was a little girl with a mop of stringy dark hair. Their heads sagged down as the child cried.

Clutching her stomach, the woman coughed. With each hacking cough, a thin stream of blood poured from her lips. She collapsed, falling on her side as red trickled from her nose and the corners of her now empty eyes. The little girl threw herself over the body, wailing in despair.

In the street, a black horse-drawn wagon pulled along a pile of corpses covered in red-dotted white sheets. A man stood on the corner, crying out and catching the momentary attention of passers-by. Snow fell in thick flakes from the dreary gray sky, combined with flecks of ash from the nearest crematorium.

"The Kai'Zi are responsible for this terrible plague that is laying waste to our land!" the man shouted, ringing a small bell. "They are the cause of our pain and suffering! Join His Majesty's Army to make them pay!"

A rangy young dark-haired man walked up to him. "How do I join the army, sir? I've lost my wife to the plague. We were newlyweds. I'd love to personally send some Kai'Zi to hell."

"Do you see that red door across the street? Knock there. They'll examine you to see if you are in good enough health for battle."

Once the carriage passed on its way to the crematorium

piping up billows of smoke down the road, the young man eagerly ran across the gray stone street toward the door, followed by a newly orphaned teenage boy.

The Island

Twelve-year-old Mia walked along the beach, her hand curled around a carved spear, her bare feet sinking into the cool sand as it oozed up between her toes. She was supposed to be catching fish, but got lost in thought as she gazed out with her pale blue eyes at the glittering ocean that seemed to never end. The ever-present glowing white arch dominated the northern half of the sky. When Mia's oldest sister, Lata, was still alive, she taught Mia that the giant sunlit arch was part of a ring that circled all around the middle of the earth, and they were just south of it. The God of All sat on top of the ring, sliding to whatever part of it he pleased to watch the people he had created down on the ground. No matter how much Mia looked toward the top edge of that massive arch, she could never actually see the God of All perched up there. How nice it would be if she could sit on the edge with him, legs dangling over the arch. What an incredible view he must have.

A breeze came off the water and whipped against Mia's sun-bronzed skin and through her short silver-white hair. Her simple dingy dress rippled around her lean body.

"Mia!" Mother shouted from somewhere inside the palm trees and green brush that backed the sun-washed beach. "You're supposed to be catching us some damned fish, not daydreaming! Get to work!"

Mia waded out into the cool water. With a well-practiced hand, she speared four shiny fish and threw them, still flopping, into her woven basket. The fifth fish eluded her as she raced back and forth, searching the water. If she came back with only four fish, her parents, her brother Deto, and her sister Sireh would eat tonight. She wouldn't.

"Mia!" Mother yelled again in that grating, belligerent voice. "Father has the fire ready! Get back over here!"

No dinner for Mia tonight. She sighed and hung her head down as she carried the basket of fresh fish down the well-worn path into the shade under the palm fronds. The rest of the family had already gathered around that evening's fire. Mother sat on a log in her dirt-stained white dress, her long hair falling in messy gray-streaked brown corkscrews around her scowling face. Beside her was Father, his beard long and thick, his brown hair tangled into dreadlocks from his not combing it in years. Across from them were Mia's teenage brother and sister, who both had Mother's brunette curls and round cheeks. As usual, Sireh did not speak to Mia. She turned her nose up and sniffed primly when Mia crouched down beside her.

Father took the fish from the basket and roasted them one at a time on a skewer, sprinkling them with dried herbs before handing them to the family members. Mia was left empty-handed except for a cut coconut. Her stomach growled so hard she felt sick, clutching it and bending over as her parents and siblings stripped the fish's flesh from the bones with their teeth.

Tired of being at the bottom of the family's dinnertime pecking order, Mia finally dared to speak up. "Mother? Father? Why is it that if we don't have enough food, I'm the one left to starve?"

"Because you're the youngest, and because Father says so," Mother growled. "Now shut up."

"Be calm," Father instructed his wife as she gritted her teeth. "While there's still a smidgen of daylight, I'm catching a fish for Mia."

"But..."

"There is no reason the child should starve." Father took the spear and the basket. His footsteps crunched through the fine-grained white beach sand. Between the trunks of the palm trees, the sun spread over the horizon like a runny egg yolk. The sunset dissipated through the semitransparent white ring, turning part of it pink.

"Thank you, Father!" Mia said, hugging her father as he returned with a long, heavy, succulent fish. After he cooked it and handed it to Mia, the fire-touched flesh tasted delicious. If it weren't for her father's small acts of kindness that sometimes won over his wife's protests, Mia may not have survived this long.

"We'll be rescued yet," Mother said to her husband as they finished their meal. "I'm sure of it."

"Frankly, my dear, I don't see it happening. They should have come for us years ago."

After the sun went down, the family retired into their makeshift dwellings near the fire, structures with thatched roofs and sides made of layered sticks. Mother and Father slept in one, Sireh and Deto shared another, and Mia had her own. The original dwellings, made from broken ship parts, had blown away a few years ago in a violent hurricane. The family kept their most treasured riches in a burlap sack buried under a thicket of nearby vegetation to protect them from storms. A few other pieces of the ship remained scattered around, including a couple of defensive cannons.

Unable to sleep, Mia slid out of her sailcloth blanket and crept out silently toward the beach nearby, with the type of softly rolling footstep that made no sound. The stars were exceptionally brilliant, diamonds glittering in the sky. They twinkled on and off as the ridged ring glowed, outshining the moon. Mia sat down, hugging her knees, and thought as she looked out at the black-and-white sky.

Whatever lay beyond the confines of this island, Mia's parents had said very little about. Focused on surviving the present, they usually refused to talk about the past. All she knew about their original home was that it had a lot of cows and trees and that the God of All watched them there from the celestial ring, just as he looked down at the island. Mother and Father's first three children, Lata, Sireh, and Deto, came with them on the ship that wrecked, though they were young at the time and did not remember much about their lives before the disaster. Mia was born on the island after the wreck.

Lata, the firstborn, fell on a bed of unstable rocks and broke her leg at the age of fourteen. The bone pierced out of the flesh of her thigh. Father tried to set the bone and bound the leg in cloth bandages. Lata grew feverish and delirious in the days following the accident, and then died. She was buried in the soil of a little-visited spot on the island. Mia, who was six at the time, still missed Lata, her favorite sibling who had taken the time to look after her, play with her, and teach her how to read. Occasionally, Mother and Father still yelled at Mia, blaming her for Lata's death. Mia knew the accusations were irrational; she did not see the accident and never laid eyes on the injury until the crying Lata had already been carried back to the family's sleeping area, leg wrapped up in bloodstained cloth. But the insinuation that Mia was somehow responsible still hurt deeply and made her question herself.

Ships never came close enough to notice the family's signal fires and rescue them. Mia's parents had confirmed that there were other land masses in the world, bigger ones, but she could barely imagine it. She only could guess what life on other soil might be like from her few children's books, and she had no way of knowing if the rivers, snow-capped mountains, and jungles in the stories were real or a product of the author's imagination. Mia wished that she could get up on that ring around the earth and see the rest of the world. Her heart ached to get off this island. With no land visible nearby, the hopes were dim that her feet would ever touch another shore. Here Mia was born, and here she would die.

Mia usually did not let herself cry, but a tear trickled down her dirty cheek tonight. She wiped it away.

After finally going to sleep, one of Mia's recurring dreams came to visit her. The walls gently gleamed, and outside the window, the dim twilight sun glittered off the white, flawless surface of the world. An ornate jade water fountain ran continuously. Mia shrank and looked up in awe. A grown-up version of herself, snowy silver hair long and held back with huge jeweled clips, looked down and smiled at Mia as she plucked the strings of a harp. The adult Mia wore a glossy white dress and a necklace of massive, beautiful sapphire jewels. How nice it would be to grow up into this graceful dream version of herself.

∞∞∞

After rising in the morning, Mia ate a breakfast of carved coconut flesh and the family trekked to the fern-surrounded freshwater spring, past a row of steaming holes in the soft grassy ground. They bent down with wooden baskets and flasks to gather water.

After being allowed a small cup of water, Mia went off to explore and play. She knew every inch of the island after years of climbing the grassy upward slopes and grasping the thick low-lying roots and vines. There was a dip in the middle of the island, and then came another slope to climb and descend. Bright yellow and orange birds shrieked and fluttered from the treetops. Once she reached the east side of the island, Mia went into her cave concealed in the pore-filled black rock, the only place her family didn't seem to know about. They rarely crossed to this shore, and Mia was glad for the privacy. A burlap sack held her rag doll and her books. She carefully guarded the books especially, since her parents considered her too old for them and would use them as fire kindling if they knew she still had them.

Mia climbed down from the cave and sat on a log on the sugar-white beach, opening her favorite leather-bound book. The parchment pages were hand-lettered and the rich illustrations hand-inked. The three child heroes rode a raft down a wide channel of water called The Great Parem River. At the front of the raft, an oil lamp hung on a hook to give them more visibility at night. The children saw exotic birds, beasts, and warriors with loincloths and spears peeking out from the jungle that flanked the river.

A raft. Mia had turned the idea over in her head from time to time. Likely too farfetched, but perhaps this was how they could get off the island. She had no idea how far a raft would go, or whether they actually floated like the one in the story did. With its flat design, a raft did not seem like it should stay above water, so Mia never thought to try building one before. That, and Mia's parents said they weren't going anywhere without a ship. But trying was better than doing nothing.

If a raft did, in fact, stay up, then this eastern beach was probably the safest place from which to paddle away. Here, an offshore reef kept the waves gentle and small; while elsewhere on the island, they crashed violently just off the beaches.

Carefully, Mia studied the illustrations of the raft in her book, which looked like sawed logs lashed together. After hiding the book away in her cave, she set about looking for materials. Finding them was not so easy. There were downed coconut trees, but she needed to find some way to saw the long, skinny trunks and attach them. Most of the larger logs were too thick to roll or carry.

The earth rumbled, and then calmed. Earthquakes had gotten more regular. The family didn't have any idea what caused them, but they had learned to mostly ignore them. After a moment's surprise, Mia refocused and continued looking around. She found two ideal-looking partial trunks from fallen trees, dragged them toward her cave, and hauled them in. Maybe she wouldn't put the whole family on the raft. Maybe she would take a solo exploratory trip and then come back and get them if she found another land mass. She decided to hold off on telling anyone about her plan unless the experimental trip proved successful. When Mia came back, triumphant and ready to rescue them, they would kiss her feet instead of looking down on her. But if she told them now, they would chastise her that her ideas were silly. And then she might never find the motivation to finish the raft, or could face criticism and ridicule if her plan failed.

The next day, Mia set about doing the same work, hunting for tree trunks. This time she quietly took her father's sharp obsidian axe with her, and she hacked away at the edges of the fallen trunks to blunt their edges and get them all about the same length. She gathered dried palm fronds and, using a technique she'd perfected over the years, hand-wove them into lengths of brown twine. To make an oar shaped like the one in her book, Mia bent a long green stick into a loop at one end and spread a layer of green palm fronds inside the loop, finishing the assembly with twine. When she was done for the day, Mia tucked all of the evidence of her project away in the cave along with the axe and set back up and down the island's slopes, across the rich green sunlight-dotted ground.

Mia stopped when someone else's footsteps approached. Her older brother Deto stepped out in front of her, dressed in his ratty tunic and hose. His eyes were cold and he smelled of unwashed armpits.

"What do you think you're doing out here?" he demanded.

"I'm just taking a walk. I'm heading back to camp."

"Not just yet, you aren't."

"I am. Now let me through, Deto." She stepped to the side and he did so just as quickly to block her.

"I need just a little favor before I can do that."

"And what's that?"

Deto gripped Mia's slender wrists in his hands. "I want a kiss."

"I can't kiss you!" Mia cried as she began trying in vain to wrench out of his grip.

"Why not?"

"Because you're my brother!"

"What's wrong with that?"

"Brothers and sisters don't marry! Let me go! Now!"

"Well, who else am I going to kiss, stuck in the middle of nowhere? Now get down!"

Before Mia could react, Deto pushed her on her back onto the mossy ground. Sharp rocks bit at her. He held down her struggling arms and legs with his and forced a disgusting, slimy kiss on her mouth, which brought her to the verge of vomiting. Her body bucked harder, trying to get free. Just as Deto shifted his position, one of Mia's legs slid out from underneath his and she rammed her knee up between his legs as hard as she could.

Deto screamed, rolled away, and curled into a ball, tears at the corners of his eyes as he clutched his groin in agony. Before he could recover, Mia ran back in the direction of the camp to tell her parents what he had done.

She found them poking at the smoldering coals in the fire pit.

"Mother! Father! Deto held me down and kissed me!" Mia panted, out of breath.

"What?" Mother said shortly. Both she and Father looked up.

"I said, Deto held me down and kissed me. It was disgusting!"

"That's preposterous," Father grumbled. "He'd do no such thing."

"Yes, he did!"

"He did not," Father barked. "I know my son! You want to get in trouble for lying, young lady?"

"I'm not lying!"

"I demand that you stop this nonsense right now!" Father ordered. Today, his eyes were as soulless as Deto's. He was not on Mia's side after all.

Deto appeared, walking a bit bowlegged. "Mother, Father," he complained in a voice still a bit strained from his pain. "Mia kicked me in a... very delicate spot."

"How could she?" Mother sympathized. Both parents stood up and ran over to hold and comfort their son. "Why did she do this to you?"

"Simply because the little brat wanted to."

"The child is acting out more and more," Mother mused.

"We do need to rectify this."

Mia stormed away from the campsite, holding back her tears.

"You get back over here right now!" her father shouted. Both parents ran after her, threw their arms around her, and dragged her back to the camp.

Mia did not let anyone see her tears during the whipping that followed. She kept her face pressed close to the palm trunk that her father used for punishments, her wrists tied together on the other side, her back exposed. After bedtime that night, Mia could not lie on her sore stinging back and had to stay on her side. Boiling inside with anger, Mia decided that she finished that raft, and if it stayed afloat, she would sneak off by herself. And no, she wouldn't be coming back for this wretched family. They could stay behind on the island until they were cobwebbed skeletons for all she cared. Even Father, since he had let her down and held the whip.

Mia's rage spurred action. She slipped out of the thatched-roof tent and silently tiptoed away into the night. The light from the ring, moon, and stars illuminated her way to the secret cave on the other side. Mia did what she could that night, dragging away trunks, hacking at them, and weaving and twisting twine as she sat outside on a black rock.

The next two nights, she did the same, making a lot of progress on the raft. However, on the third night of work, she stopped chopping with the axe when heavy footsteps crashed through the brush nearby.

"Hello?" called out Father's groggy voice. "Who's there?"

Heart pounding, Mia ducked into the trees and then climbed up to her cave as fast as she could. She peered around the edges as Father stepped out onto the glowing silver beach, rubbing his eyes and glancing around in the light of the small oil lamp he held. "Hello?"

Mia held her breath nervously as he paced up and down the beach. She could not be sure if he had noticed her footprints or the makings of the raft by the time he stumbled back into the trees and toward the camp.

After returning to her small thatched-roof hut, it took a lot of willpower for the tired Mia to wake up in the morning. A bitter soup boiled in the iron cauldron that hung from twine over the coals of the fire. As the family drank from carved bowls, Father prodded at the few possessions he had dug up from his underground stash, a bejeweled ring and an elaborate gilded pendant from better, wealthier times.

When breakfast was done, Mia escaped into the trees and into the dip in the center of the island. In her state of exhaustion, Mia fell asleep on the soil in the protective shade of the trees. She was jolted half-awake when something rustled and tugged at her body.

"Take it off," her brother's detached voice said.

Mia sat up and found her dress pushed up underneath her arms, exposing her chest and underpants.

Deto reached for her again, grabbing at the rumpled dress. "Take your clothes off."

"No!" Mia screamed.

"Take them off! Or I'll rat you out again, tell Mother and Father you've kicked me in the jewels."

Mia wrenched free of Deto's grasp as her dress fabric ripped loudly. She ran as fast as she could. Deto followed hot on her trail. After hearing a loud thud behind her, she looked over her shoulder. Deto groaned on all fours on the ground, having tripped over a root. Mia took this opportunity to get further ahead. She found a large tree with great roots above the ground and low branches, and scrambled up into it.

"Mia?" Deto called after he got up off the ground, brushing dirt off himself and pacing around, looking from side to side. "Mia? Where are you, you brat? Where did you go?"

She peeked down from between the broad leaves of the tree as he walked right under her. She held her breath and tried not to make the tiniest move.

Eventually Deto gave up the search and stormed off, swearing under his breath. Mia took refuge in the tree for a while longer before she finally felt safe descending to the ground. She was especially determined to get away from here now. She vowed to finish the raft and sail off into the unknown tonight.

∞ ∞ ∞

That evening, it rained hard, and the family crouched in their manmade shacks to eat a dinner of cold dried jerky made from the flesh of tarniks, the small striped tree animals inhabiting the island. Another earthquake briefly rumbled. Mia's mother scolded her for tearing her dress earlier that day and getting it so dirty, and ordered her to mend the rip herself with a needle and thread. As she sat sewing by the light of her small oil lamp, Mia realized that the heavy pattering rain was a blessing in disguise. The background noise would conceal the cracks of Father's stolen axe hitting wood, and she could do much of the work in the dry cave.

Again, Mia waited until everyone else extinguished their lamps. And then she crept out of her tent, planning for tonight's escape. She would need food on the raft, so she raided the family food stores, which they kept underneath a protective thatched overhang. Mia tucked away several strips of jerky, a few coconuts, a water canteen, and a knife into a sack. She also decided to bring the oil lamp just in case, even though she could see quite well in the dark. Food sack slung over her back and lamp in hand, Mia began a difficult ascent up the wet slope, her feet sinking and slipping in the mud. Making it to the other beach took longer than usual as the rain shellacked Mia's dress and hair to her face and body. The clouds obscured the stars, moon, and ring. How could the God of All see people when rainclouds hid the earth from his view? Would he not find out that she was committing a sin in abandoning her stranded, shipwrecked family? She tried to push the thoughts out of her mind—even if the God of All sent her to hell for this, she had come too far now to stop her plan.

Mia climbed into her cave and set the lamp down. She had almost enough logs, but probably needed one or two more. Maybe a bit more twine as well. With the black-bladed obsidian axe in hand, she went back out into the sheets of rain to search for more wood. She found a washed-up log just the right width on the beach and began to chop at the outer edges. She rolled it up into the cave and then set to work looking for another.

Suddenly, a dark human form stumbled out of the trees, holding up a lamp, a blurry orange star in the wetness.

"Mia!" Father's voice boomed. "Where are you? Your brother checked your bed and he said that you were gone! We are in a panic. Please come out!"

Mother followed close behind, shaking mud from her feet and the bottom of her long sopping-wet dress. They both turned directly to face her as she stood out in the open on the gritty wet beach sand.

"Mia, get over here right now!" Mother ordered. They headed straight toward her, fast and angry. Mia closed her eyes and wished hard that she could just be invisible right now, surrounded by some sort of magical protective bubble that would hide her from view. She'd never escape. She was caught, and she resigned herself to another punishment, and lifelong imprisonment to follow.

"Wait, where did she go?" Mother said.

Mia dared to open her eyes a slit as Father's head suddenly whipped from side to side in confusion.

"I could have sworn that I saw a figure, and her eyes," Mother grumbled.

They walked past her, so close she could have reached out and touched them, as they shook their heads.

"I was certain I saw the glint in her eyes too," Father pointed out. "How could she be gone like this?"

Mia's parents paced from side to side, shouting out her name. When their backs were turned, Mia ran to her cave at the fastest pace she could muster. She peeked out, panting as they searched the beach and the nearby trees for her.

How had they not seen or grabbed her when she had been standing right in front of them? How had they passed her? She'd gotten lucky. This time.

Mia did not want to know what might have happened if she was asleep in her enclosure when her brother crawled in.

Mother complained, wiping rain out of her eyes as they passed close to the cave. Mia could not make out all of her words as the rain pounded down, though she heard "that small brat" somewhere in there.

"What else were we going to do with her? Smother her?" Father replied. He was standing closer and Mia could more easily hear him. "Perhaps we should have. I don't think we ought to bring her back, even if rescuers do arrive. I know we've been unsure, but let's face it, we need to do something about the girl."

"Let us get back to bed before we catch our deaths of cold, and we'll look for her in the morning. Perhaps the problem will take care of itself, with this sort of weather."

Mia, too scared to move, squatted just behind the cave entrance and watched the beach outside long after Mother and Father were out of view, their voices out of earshot. The rain died down and then cleared up. The clouds parted, allowing pure light to descend on the beach from the great white ring and the stars. After listening hard for any noises in the trees, Mia got back to work on her raft, trying to be quiet. After working with some of the dried palm fronds she had stockpiled in the cave, she came up with enough twine to lash all of the logs together. She did so as tightly and securely as she could, weaving the twine between the logs so that it looked much like the picture in her favorite book and securing it with knots she had learned to do by herself, nearly impossible to untie.

Now it was time. After looking carefully around the beach for signs of her family, Mia began the laborious process of sliding the raft out of the cave. It made more noise than she would have liked as it scraped across the rock. She grabbed the ax, lamp, food sack, handmade palm-frond oar, and small sack of prized possessions and stacked them on top of the raft. She pushed it slowly across the soggy beach into a nearby cove of shallow water as the rain-cooled air made her cheeks tingle. As it entered the water, Mia prayed that it would float, but waited for it to sink and disappoint her, proving a floating raft to simply be a fantasy in a children's book.

For now, it was staying afloat. That could always change when Mia jumped on top.

Mia waded out of the cove and off the beach until the water came up to her waist, holding on to the raft, and then she decided it was time. As she threw her body and leg on, the raft rocked violently, the water splashing over the side, and she knew then that it would sink. She grabbed for her two sacks and hung on for dear life.

It was a miracle. Except for her foot, all of Mia was on the raft. And it was floating. Aimlessly floating in one place, but floating nonetheless. Carefully, she pulled the remaining foot on board, sat up, and then smiled wide. She paddled from one side to the other with the oar, guessing at the motions from the children going down the river in the book illustrations. The raft glided across the water with a thrilling ease of motion, leaving a faint rippled wake behind. After figuring out the most efficient way to do so, she paddled as fast as she could. A couple of waves rolled up, splashing over the front of the raft, but she stayed up nonetheless.

Mia was going to get out of here. She was free.

After paddling out some distance, Mia glanced over her shoulder. Her island home was just a shaggy black outline on the star-filled horizon. It was all she had ever known. She would never see her cave, her trees, her black rocks, the spring, the silky beaches, or the steaming vents again. She was suddenly very scared. There was no way of knowing what, if anything, was out there. What if the waters teemed with the man-eating sharks her parents talked about from time to time? What if she was making a terrible mistake and the ocean stretched on and on for longer than she had the supplies for? What if other islands were dangerous places? What if she ended up stranded and starved? What if her raft broke out here and she sunk? Mia's head swam with so many terrifying what-ifs that she almost aborted her mission and turned around.

Mia reminded herself then of the way her family treated her—being hit, whipped, talked down to, and ignored. "Dumb as a rock," "can't do anything right," and "didn't come out right" were among the phrases regularly used to describe her, words that hurt. The last conversation she had overheard between her parents hinted that they may have even wanted her dead. And then there was the sister who refused to speak to or look at her and the brother who had attacked her.

There had to be something better out in the unknown world. In Mia's books, people were happy and treated each other kindly. Mia turned her head forward. She paddled and took deep breaths. In her sleep-deprived state, her eyes began to slam shut, but she forced herself to stay awake—she had to get far enough away that her parents wouldn't see her out on the water when they went looking for her in the morning. Mia's stomach growled, but she refrained from snacking, wanting to make her rations of food last. As she paddled, she went into a sort of trance and her mind wandered. She slipped into the fantasy palace she had crafted in her mind when she was small, with glittering snow, stunning white-capped mountains, velvet curtains, reindeer hides, and intricate stone carvings. Ethereal music came from a harp, like the one her grown-up self played in some of her dreams. Mother always did say Mia had too wild of an imagination; she'd never seen snow in her life. She only knew what it was from one of the books and a few of the bedtime stories Lata, Mia's deceased sister, used to tell her when she was small.

Mia grew delirious from exhaustion as her arms wore out. She took a break and put the oar down in front of her. Straight ahead, the sun was starting to come up just behind the ring, turning the few fluffy clouds on the eastern horizon lavender. Mia looked over her shoulder. The island was just a dot now, and she was too tired to go on. She curled on the round logs under her sailcloth blanket and instantly fell asleep, wrapping her arms around her supplies.

When Mia woke, the sun was high in the sky, reflecting blinding sparkles off the deep blue water. She sat up on the raft that still carried her, rubbed her eyes, and let herself have a snack of tarnik jerky and thick sweet water from a cut-open coconut. She wished she could just eat the whole bag of food. Mia carved the flesh out of the coconut and ravenously downed that too. And then she pushed herself to keep paddling. If she made sure to keep track of the sun and the great ring in the sky and go east, she had to get somewhere eventually. As the sun eventually set and the stars, ring, and faint moon lit up, Mia passed the time talking to herself out loud. The wind picked up, and a salted breeze beat against her face. In this endless water that all looked the same, it was hard to tell how much, if any, progress she made.

The second day out on the water, Mia again woke up close to noon. Now bright pink, her skin felt tender and raked with salt from the surrounding ocean. She was terribly thirsty and poked another coconut with the knife, draining the water out into her mouth as it dribbled down her chin. She only had one coconut left after this, and the water canteen she was trying to save for last. If only she could just drink all the water in the ocean. But Mother and Father said that the salt would kill a person, and that was why the family relied on coconut water and the freshwater spring.

A lump unexpectedly came up in Mia's throat at the thought of never seeing her parents again, or not for a very long time. They'd had their cruel moments, but deep down she still wanted their approval and wanted to see them smile.

Dark forms slithered through the surrounding sapphire waters. A gray fin silently broke the surface. Mia instantly knew what those things were, circling just under the surface. Man-eating sharks. Frantically she started to paddle faster, hoping to outrun the deadly fang-jawed fish.

A faint rumbling noise growled from the distance. As Mia peeked over her shoulder, a gray plume of smoke rose over the horizon of water. What on earth was that? The cloud grew as Mia paddled even faster in her fear, not wanting to find out. The sharks continued to circle the raft and Mia kept her legs tucked tightly underneath her dress, trying not to think about them. As it had yesterday, the wind started to press against her.

Mia paddled after nightfall despite her aching arms, taking breaks to gobble strips of jerky to satisfy her clamoring stomach. Clouds gathered in the sky, joining up and turning the world darker. And then it started raining, the drops creating little circles on the surface of the ocean. At first, the drops felt refreshing on Mia's sunburned skin, but when she got cold, she took refuge by emptying one of her supply sacks into the other and hiding inside the empty sack. The wind began to whistle around Mia, harder and harder, as the raft rocked to and fro. When a wave crashed over it, wetting the surface, Mia clung to her things as hard as she could, frightened that the storm could sink her. The rain began to pour down violently, pounding against the wood and soaking everything. It was relentless, with no sign of letting up.

Mia decided to start paddling through the waves, which now crested higher and higher. Hopefully this storm would be over soon. The rain and waves slammed into her as the raft bounced up and crashed back down. Lightning zigzagged across the dark, tumultuous sky.

A huge wave rose right in front of Mia, curved, its top frothing. The raft rode up it, going sideways. And then the wave crashed down right on top of Mia, knocking her upside down. She didn't know where she was or which direction she was going as the water forced her down deep beneath its surface. She swam against the bubbles rushing against her skin until her head broke the surface of the black-looking water. Gasping frantically for air, she looked around for her raft. A near-blinding flash of lightning streaked the sky overhead and illuminated the water, showing a raft longer whole. Logs floated every which way, and so did a few of Mia's possessions. Most of the food had already sunk, as did her beloved books.

Mia swam through the roiling, frothy water and grasped one log. They were knocked so far apart it was futile to try to reassemble the raft again. Clinging to that lone log, she started to cry.

Something floated past with a strap waving behind it. The water canteen. Mia swam toward that and grabbed it. Her legs kicked underneath the water as the waves slammed into her face, threw her backwards, and left her spitting and her eyes burning. Her leg brushed against something big, long, and slimy beneath the surface. A man-eating shark! Petrified, Mia began to kick harder.

By the time the fierce storm finally died and day broke in the parting fluffy pink clouds, Mia was exhausted and could barely move. But falling asleep meant death, letting go of the log and helplessly drowning. If she wanted to live, she had to stay awake as long as she could. Despite her chest-gripping fear of sharks in the water, Mia stopped swimming for a rest and gulped half of the crystal-clear water from the canteen. She put the cork back in to save the rest for later. Her eyes began to close against her will again, and she resigned herself to the fact that she would probably not get out of the ocean alive. She should have never gone on this foolish endeavor.

It was now high noon, not a cloud in the sky anymore, and sleep and certain death were not far off. Mia's dried, cracked lips longed for more water. Weakly, she drained the rest from the canteen, and then dropped it in her surprise when an irregularity appeared in the water.

What was that humongous, dark, mechanical-looking thing with the pointed profile on top? That was a ship! It might be too far away for the crew to hear Mia's cries for help, but she tried anyway.

"Help!" she screamed at the top of her lungs, her throat scratchy. "Help!"

The ship continued on to wherever it was going, now a bit further away. But Mia did not want to give up. "Help!" she screamed until her voice was hoarse, praying to the God of All that the ship would notice her and projecting her mind outward in its direction.

When she was just about to let go of hope for her survival, the ship slowly turned, and then headed straight toward Mia. She called out and waved an arm as the wooden contraption grew bigger. A smaller boat detached from the side of the ship and approached her. As it drew closer, Mia spotted a figure in a brown cloak, paddling with two wooden oars. Bright red hair peeked out from inside the hood. The stranger reached down, grasped Mia under the arms, and pulled her up into the little wooden boat. Her legs buckled underneath her, drained of their strength. She curled on the floor of the boat.

"What were you doing out there, little girl?" the red-haired man asked her in a resonant voice with a strange lilting accent different from her family's. "My goodness, the sun has burnt you good."

"I wanted to... see the world."

"That's what we're doing out here—we wanted to see the ocean, the whales and dolphins. But shouldn't you be in a ship too, rather than just swimming? You could have been a shark's meal."

"I... had... a raft. Then... it broke."

"A raft? In that storm last night?! I'm not sure how we spotted you at this distance. You're very fortunate. Where is your family?"

"On an island," Mia weakly mumbled.

"Where is the island?"

"Um… west of here."

"Why weren't they with you?"

"They were… rather cruel. But… maybe… you should go get them."

The little boat was lifted on hooks at the side of the ship, drawn by ropes. The cloaked man who had rescued Mia carried her on board and rested her on the wood planks. A crimson-haired, freckle-faced woman ran to Mia's side and knelt down, her gray dress puddling at her feet. She propped Mia's head on a pillow and brought a flask of water to her cracked lips. How strange to be seeing people not of her family. And their hair, so red, like no hair Mia had ever seen before. The woman left, returned with a bowl, and rubbed a cooling poultice onto Mia's painful, reddened skin.

"What is your name, child?" the woman asked.

"Mia."

"Mia, my name is Terni. What's your surname?"

"What is a surname?"

"Your last name."

"I'm not sure. I… I don't think I have any other names."

"How old are you?"

"Twelve."

The redheaded woman turned and talked to someone else. "She looks like she's spent her entire life in the sun. My, how sun-bleached that hair is. It's almost like an old woman's."

When she had the strength to stand, Mia was led by passengers to a small room below deck. She sat on the bed, covered with a beautifully patterned wool blanket. The down mattress softly sank below her. As the woman gave her a bowl of soup floating with bits of meat, Mia looked around in amazement at the room. It had a small round window. Outside, the blue water gently waved past. The walls were made of wood planks. A huge oil lamp rested on the nightstand. After a simple life on the island, she felt a sense of wonder, yet also got anxious at being closed in.

Later, the ship's captain, a tall man with a long white

beard, came in to see Mia. He sat down beside her on the bed and asked about her name, family, and origins. As she gave the captain their names—she only knew her siblings' first names; not Mother's or Father's—and mentioned her eldest sister buried on the island, she realized just how little she really knew about her family and their lives before the shipwreck.

"Where were they from? Where is their home country?"

"I don't know."

"Why did you construct this raft and leave by yourself?"

"I wanted to see what was outside of the island. And I went through difficulties with my family. But now..." Tears pooled in Mia's eyes. No matter how they had treated her, she hoped they were alive.

"Mia, m'dear, can you describe the island for me? What did the land look like?"

"It was odd... sort of like a bowl. There were lots of trees and lots of sand on the beaches. And a few caves in big black rocks. The sides of the island sort of rose up. And then there was a dip in the middle."

"Was there any steam issuing forth from this island?"

"Yes. There were a few little holes in the ground letting out steam."

"Did the ground ever shake?"

"Yes. It was happening more and more."

"Child, we did see one island west of here. We were not close to it. We saw it erupt, unfortunately."

"Erupt?"

"It was a volcano."

"A mountain that explodes with heat?" Lata, Mia's sister, had told her about those once.

"As far as we could tell. Though it was at quite a distance, we saw the cloud of ash. We were very lucky that we got away from it when we did, and that the ash headed in the opposite direction."

Could that have been the island she'd left her family behind on? Were they all dead and burned now?

"You saw no other islands?"

"No, I'm afraid. But it's possible there are others and the volcano was not the one where your family's stranded."

"Can't we go back and check?" Mia cried.

"I'm very sorry, child, I'm afraid we can't do that. It is dangerous to go near a volcano, in case it is still spewing, and this is a leisure vessel. It's not equipped for that sort of mission. Right now, we're headed back to Dakoris. As soon as we reach the harbor I will arrange to send a rescue mission out to search for your family."

"Dakoris?" Mia had never heard of that place before.

"Our home."

After she was left alone in the room, Mia told herself she ought to be grateful for her timely rescue by this ship full of benevolent strangers, but the thought of her family dead, drowned in red lava, haunted her. And the strangers on the ship frightened and overwhelmed her with their loud voices and the odd way they dressed. She cried herself to sleep in the bed that night.

"Mia," said a soft voice from behind her as someone shook her shoulder. It was Terni, the woman who had given her water and rubbed the cooling poultice on her skin as soon as she was pulled onto the ship. Dim light filtered through the round portal window. "Mia, get up. There's something out there that I think will delight you."

"What is it?" she mumbled, feeling like she could sleep for another ten hours.

"The largest school of koti dolphins we've seen yet. Have you ever seen a dolphin?"

"No."

"Now's your chance. It is breathtaking. I have a fresh dress for you to wear, hanging beside the door."

Terni closed the door to give Mia some privacy as she changed clothes. Mia followed Terni to the deck of the gently rocking vessel. Her stomach turned. An awed crowd was gathered at the edge railing in the pink dawn light.

Mia found a gap in the crowd and peeked out at the water, boiling with finned creatures. One giant animal, looking like a sort of fish, jumped clean out of the water, followed by another like it. Their skin gleamed and continuously changed color, pulsating splotches going from red to purple to blue. They opened their long snouts ridged with sharp teeth and made chittering noises. Their arc ended. They splashed back into the water as others began to jump.

They looked so frightening, no less grotesque than man-eating sharks. Mia had never seen or heard of such a bizarre, toothy creature. She shrieked, turned, and ran bare-footed back across the cool dewy wood of the deck as the voyagers turned to stare.

"The poor dear, she's just been through a lot," Terni explained as she quickly followed Mia to comfort her.

Dakoris

Mia stood at the ship's wooden railing, resting her hands on it and looking outward at the noon sky, where the great white celestial arch was now smaller but still filled up much of the north. Over the past several days she had seen more colorful koti dolphins and two great whales, and she'd stopped being afraid of them, learning to admire even the massive species of whale that looked like it could take a bite out of the ship if it wanted to. She had bathed with a bucket of warm water, and after several applications of the cooling poultice, her sunburn was healing. Clean and shiny, Mia's silver hair was pulled back into a clip. A few locks of it fell out and brushed her cheeks. Terni had fitted Mia with a dress and cloak. Both were just a bit too long and trailed behind her when she walked. The heavy clothing stifled her. A full, meaty meal sat heavy in Mia's belly. During the meal times, she could not get enough after all the hunger she'd suffered, and struggled to pace herself.

Terni appeared beside Mia as she stood at the rail. "You look just like a little lady," she complimented her. "Already much healthier than when we found you. Oh, look, there it is! Land!"

Low-lying land appeared on the horizon, dotted with small trees and shrubs. It looked impossibly huge, going on forever. Instead of stopping, the ship went past it and sailed into another expanse of water.

"Why didn't we stop?" Mia asked Terni. "You said that land was your home?"

"We have just passed into Dakor Bay. Tomorrow we'll be

docking at the city of Korus."

"What's Korus like?" Mia's whole body tingled with curiosity.

"It is a large city, the place where the royal family lives. A lot of wool traders make their home there. The people are warm and friendly. Have you ever seen a dog before?"

"No. My mother mentioned them once."

"You'll be seeing plenty of them. Our country is home to the Dakor Shepherd, which is the most intelligent kind of dog in the world. Outsiders will offer a lot of money for a puppy."

"I don't know what dogs look like." Mia pictured a ratlike creature with stripes like the tarnik.

"You'll see plenty soon, m'dear, once you get into the city. My husband and I are thinking of finding ourselves a dog."

They went below the deck to the dining hall for a dinner of goat stew and bread. The burly men who rowed the ship also joined them for a short time. These people had a mealtime tradition Mia had never heard of. Before they started to dine, they prayed and bowed their heads to a carved wooden figurine positioned in the center of the table. They thanked the figurine, which looked like a series of attached spheres, for each feast. It reminded Mia of how Mother and Father had occasionally looked up to the ring in the sky to express their gratitude to the God of All. Once everyone started eating, Mia again had a hard time not gulping the soup and bread down too fast. With little regard to the taste of the meal, she just wanted to eat and eat after these years of living on lean servings of tarnik, fish, and coconut and watching her siblings get priority over her.

The next day, Mia's attention was raptly fixed on the approaching coastline. Mountains dizzyingly high, taller than she could have ever imagined, rose up in abundance in the background, their craggy stone peaks patched with snow. The vegetation colors along the coast ranged from green to orange to red like blood.

"Terni," Mia asked, "what is causing those strange yellow and orange colors?"

"It's the beginning of fall, m'dear."

"What's fall?"

"It's one of the four seasons. Was there no fall on your island?"

"I'm not sure. We had just a few seasons—the wet season, the dry season, and some years there was the hurricane season."

"I believe the island was close to the equator."

"What's the equator?"

"It is an imaginary line around the center of the earth, right under the big ring. Here in Dakoris, we're well south. The further north or south you go, the colder the winters become. I don't know why that is; it's something to do with the sun. And while fall is beginning here—when the leaves fall from the trees that aren't evergreens and they go to sleep—it's spring north of the equator. That means that the leaves are growing back on the trees and flowers are blooming."

"I can't wait to see a spring season. But those orange and red and yellow trees I'm seeing... those are beautiful. I didn't know the world had trees that change colors."

"It sounds as though your parents hardly told you anything."

"They didn't tell me much. What's at the very bottom of the earth? What's at the very top?"

"Great masses of ice. It's always cold in those places. Even Dakoris will be getting cold soon. As you've spent your life on a tropical island, you'll want to bundle up and be careful."

"Will it snow?"

"Definitely."

The thought excited Mia. She wanted to feel the crystal powder of snow in her fingers, play with it, and roll it up.

The ship docked at Korus, next to a series of long wooden planks. A red flag flapped up above in the faintly chilly breeze. The passengers dismounted with their sacks of belongings and met the people waiting for them at the dock. The noise of reuniting families was almost too loud for Mia and she nearly lost track of her companion, Terni. After fearing that she'd get crushed in a throng of people, Mia found Terni in the arms of a man with curly orange hair and a large nose. Breathing quickly in her panic, Mia grasped the back of Terni's cloak, digging her fingers into the wool.

"How was your journey, my love?" the man asked Terni. "Did you see plenty of whales and dolphins?"

"Certainly. They were just stunning. It's unfortunate that you could not join me on the voyage."

"Too much business to take care of at home, and I would have found it dull, sitting around on a ship for so long and looking at water. Who is this girl?"

"It's a long story," Terni told her husband. "We found this girl in the water and rescued her. May I speak with you privately? Mia, can you wait right here? We'll be right back—don't make a move."

"But..."

Terni and her husband had already walked away. Though the crowd grew thinner, Mia was terrified, left there by herself among the bustling strangers. She caught a glimpse of Terni and her husband talking, gesturing widely with their hands and arms. It seemed to take forever. She longed for Terni to come back by her side.

At last, the couple did return. Terni took Mia's hand and spoke briefly to the ship's captain. Then she led Mia into the cobblestone streets, unbearably busy and loud with fruit vendors and merchants selling rugs with bright zigzag patterns.

"We are going to allow you to stay at our house for a few nights," Terni explained. "We cannot keep you for much longer, so we'll be looking for someone else to take you in. Don't worry, we'll put you in good hands."

Just a few nights? But Mia found herself attached to Terni, looking up to her as a new mother. She couldn't be bouncing her off to some stranger. Mia looked down, closing her eyes, because she'd had enough of the constant, nauseating, scary movement on the dock and in the streets. In groups, people sure were loud, their voices piercing.

"Oh, look!" Terni announced. "The royal family is coming!"

Thrilled at the unexpected chance to see a real-life king and queen for the first time, Mia looked up as the crowds of cloaked people moved quickly to the sidewalks. Horses' hooves clacked down the wide cobblestone lane. The thick-furred horses pulled a wheeled red carriage, something else Mia had never seen before. The king and queen of Dakoris sat on an elevated bench in the back, both wearing gilded crowns and velvet red capes. Both had red hair like almost everyone else Mia saw in this place, and the queen's was the rich color of a rose, cascading down in fancy curls over her glittering white gown.

"Wow, those really are the king and queen of Dakoris?" Mia gasped, gripping Terni's arm. The scene looked like something straight out of a fairytale.

"Yes, and sitting in front of them are the three princesses."

The princesses, two young women and a little girl, all had long red hair that sparkled with pearls and jewels. They wore identical shining pink dresses. Silk shawls, edged with diamonds, covered their arms. The royal family kept their heads high and their gaze forward. Mia was awed when they passed her, though something didn't look quite right about them. They were all too thin with sticklike arms and pasty skin. One of them looked exhausted, her eyes barely open.

"They looked almost... ill," Mia whispered to Terni in her surprise after the royal family had passed to wherever they were going.

"They try to hide it, but their health is frail," Terni said quietly. "I have a friend who works at the palace and she has told me about some of the family's struggles. They had a son, who had an illness where he would not stop bleeding once he got a cut. And then that poor boy fell down the stairs, which caused his demise. Apparently, someone from the east put a curse on the family a long time ago, dooming them to this poor health."

"You know what I think," Terni's husband cut in. "I think it's generation after generation of uncles marrying nieces, brothers marrying sisters. And the more it goes on, the sicker they get. The king and queen you just saw are half-siblings. Not only that, but cousins."

"They're brother and sister?!" Mia exclaimed. "Mother and Father said that brothers and sisters aren't supposed to marry. But my brother kept chasing me. I suppose he wanted to marry me, or something."

"In some countries, it's frowned upon," Terni informed her. "But here, they want to keep the royal bloodline as pure as they can, so they don't want to marry outsiders. I'm still not sure that's what's making them sick, though."

Terni, her husband, and Mia walked the rest of the way to their house. Stone houses were set well back from the street behind iron fences, and hardly anyone was out, bringing much-needed peace and quiet for Mia. Brilliant orange and crimson leaves floated down from the trees. As they passed one residence, a spotted gray monster with huge, demonic ears and clawed feet suddenly charged out from behind the house and came straight at Mia, sharp teeth exposed. The thing let out sharp shrieking noises as it clanged against the fence, intent on killing Mia. Her face went completely white and she bolted. Her cloak almost came off.

"Mia!" Terni cried. "Get back here!"

"It's a monster!" Mia wailed as Terni chased her. She caught up to Mia, wrapping her in her arms.

"It's a dog," Terni soothed. "It's the Dakor Shepherd, the breed I was telling you about. It just got startled by us passing by."

"That's what a dog looks like?" Mia asked in a trembling voice. "It looks absolutely frightening."

"They're very friendly once you get to know them, m'dear. They're just protective of their land."

"But... but... I don't want to get to know a dog! Why would anyone want to keep one? With those hideous fangs, those sharp claws... people must have a death wish!"

For some reason Mia couldn't understand, Terni suddenly

started laughing. "Wait until a dog rolls over and gives you that pleading look for you to scratch his belly."

"I am never scratching the belly of any creature that has those killer fangs," Mia insisted.

A few houses down from where the vicious pet monster lived, they reached Terni's home. After closing the gate behind them, they walked down a tree-lined path. The brightly colored fallen leaves crunched softly under Mia's leather moccasins. Mia had to take another wide-eyed look around before she was led inside. The heavy wooden door was closed behind her and latched shut with an iron hook. A fire crackled in the brick fireplace, and most of the furniture was draped with the patterned wool blankets and rugs that Mia had been seeing around since her rescue. A small spotted pointy-eared creature walked up silently and sniffed at Mia. She knew what this animal was—a cat. In one of her books that now rested at the bottom of the ocean, the main character had one as a pet. And there'd also been a couple of cats living on the ship to control the mice below deck. Mia reached down and picked up the cat, enthralled by the softness of its fur and how it vibrated, and then she dropped it, startled, when it began to knead at her with razor-sharp claws.

As Terni and her husband cooked dinner stew over the fire, Mia explored, asking about the unfamiliar tools and implements she found in the home. When she discovered a bookshelf, she took down the books and flipped through them, amazed by all the information they contained. It was hard for her to put them away when supper was ready.

Atop the round table sat another one of those carved wooden idols. Mia asked what it was for.

"It is a figure of the sheep-goddess of Dakoris," Terni explained. "If we respect the sheep-goddess, she will bring abundance and good things for the shepherds, weavers, and traders."

"Sheep?" Mia had heard that word once or twice from her parents.

"Do you know what they are?"

"Not quite."

"It's the sacred animal of Dakoris. They are covered in white wool. Their hair is dyed and woven into the rugs and blankets you've been seeing."

"Dakor wool and blankets will fetch a princely sum of money from outsiders," Terni's husband added. "We sell them for a living."

"Does the sheep-goddess live on top of the big ring in the sky?" Mia wanted to know, remembering what her oldest sister taught her about the God of All when she was little.

"Yes. She lives in the heavenly fleece that forms the ring."

Later, Mia laid down in the couple's spare bedroom, underneath a heavy, itchy wool blanket with fuchsia and blue stripes. They warmed a few stones in the fireplace and wrapped them in cloths to keep Mia's narrow bed from getting too cold. The following day, the sky was pale gray and overcast, and the air held a chilly bite. Bringing Mia along, the couple went out to the city's market square and occupied a booth, where they dangled blankets from rods and filled baskets with colorful spools of wool yarn to entice buyers. Leaving her husband behind at the booth, Terni decided to take Mia on a small walk, pointing out the places where people purchased groceries and where they bought supplies. Mia watched with interest for a while as an old gray-haired woman wove a rug on a loom by the side of the street. She couldn't figure out how a rug came out of that tall wooden contraption with strings hanging down. Her weathered fingers worked so fast they turned to blurs.

When Mia turned to go back to the booth, she could not find Terni anywhere in sight among the passersby. Concerned, she started to peek around corners. Her hood slid off her head and fell to the back of her cloak, revealing her smooth, metallic yet snowy hair.

"Hey, you," said a raspy voice from an alleyway. Mia turned, looking for its source.

"Yeah, you." An old man stood, chewing a stick with what few teeth he had left. His blue eyes raked over Mia. His face twisted into a grimace of disgust, and then he spat on her.

Mia stood in shock as the thick smelly tobacco-stained saliva trickled down the front of her cloak. Her brother Deto spat on her when they were younger, but she hadn't thought this cruel treatment by others would continue into her new life beyond the island. She turned and ran, trying not to cry.

After Mia found Terni and told her what had happened, Terni decided to go home early, leaving her husband to man the booth. Terni accompanied the distressed Mia down the more peaceful streets back to her house. As they walked, Terni suggested that Mia keep her hood up to cover her hair.

"I can't be sure why that man spat on you, but your hair does make you stand out," Terni warned Mia. "It makes you resemble a certain race that is not well-liked. Those of us who were on the ship know you cannot be one of them, because there are almost none left. This was an arctic race, and you were born on an island in the tropics. But those who do not know your story don't know any better, and they'll make assumptions from what they see."

"If people are going to believe I come from some race they don't like because of my hair color, then what do I do?" Mia asked. "Surely I can't keep it hidden all the time."

"Hair color is easy enough to change. Would you believe that I was not born with red hair? I dye my hair so that I won't stand out so much in a country filled with redheads. I know many others who do the same."

The thought of changing one's hair color just to fit in sounded silly to Mia, but she wanted her own hair dyed so that no one would spit on her anymore. When they passed the house with the white furry monster in the yard, Mia gave it a wide berth. Again, the dog lunged at the fence. Instead of barking and snarling, it let out a high-pitched whine and stared at Mia with wide eyes through the fence bars.

"That dog has become fond of you," Terni pointed out. "Why don't you scratch him behind the ears? Or give him a pet on the snout?"

"Absolutely not! I'm not going anywhere near those jaws!"

After they went inside, Terni prepared hair dye, mixing herbs with hot water in a bowl until they became green sludge. Mia couldn't figure out how this fecal-looking slime could turn hair red. After massaging the thick mixture through Mia's shoulder-length hair, Terni covered her scalp with a large rag and they sat in front of the warm fire and talked. After the dye set in, Terni took Mia outside and rinsed the grit and gel from her hair in a bucket of water. As Mia sat in front of the fire, letting her hair dry, Terni's husband came home with a sack bulging with coins from his sales.

"Go look in the mirror," Terni urged Mia shortly before dinner. "Your hair is stunning. You could pass for a native-born Dakor girl."

Mia went to the mirror in the spare bedroom, examining herself by the light of a large oil lamp. Her hair was bright red with a deep, glossy glow. The color looked a bit out of place, as her silver-white eyebrows and eyelashes did not match the hair. But they wouldn't be terribly noticeable to those who did not look closely. Having grown up with no mirrors, Mia studied her features for quite a while, getting to know how they looked from an outside perspective. She had an upturned nose. Her eyes had a slanted shape above her high cheekbones and were clear sky blue in color, not brown or mossy green like the rest of the eyes in her immediate family. The family that might now be dead.

That night Mia cried again, reflecting upon her few fond memories of them. First she focused on Lata, the sister who had broken her leg, gotten a fever, and died several years ago, leaving an emotional wound that never quite healed. And then Mia began to paint her parents in an overly rosy light, focusing on the times when they'd been kinder and more generous than normal, letting her eat extra or catching a fish for her at the last minute or deciding not to beat her. If only she had let them in on her escape plan, they'd all be alive and together today, and maybe they would treat her more kindly in their happiness over being liberated from that remote island. Then Mia remembered that she had decided to keep the raft a secret because they told her she couldn't do anything right and she knew they would shoot down any of her escape ideas too.

Yet she had escaped. Maybe they were wrong about some things.

Mia's emotions swung from love and mourning to hate and disgust as she again felt the slime of her brother's kiss and the tugging of him attempting to take her clothes off. And the obvious favoritism on the part of their parents—that she was punished severely for kicking him and freeing herself, while he saw no consequences for kissing her except for a sore crotch. And try as she might, Mia could not forget that last vicious conversation between her parents she'd overheard, that the "problem" of her existence might "take care of itself." As the memories replayed themselves in her mind, both good and bad, more confusion set in and she started to love her family again, hating herself for failing to make a raft large enough for them all.

For the next two days, Mia cautiously explored the surrounding city. Gradually, with exposure, the noise in the market square got less and less scary and a bit more bearable for Mia. Now that she had red hair, nobody gave her a second glance even when the hood of her cloak fell down in the breeze.

The evening of the second day, Mia and Terni came home to find two horses hitched outside, spotted and covered in thick fur with long white manes and tails. Mia cautiously stepped aside when one of the horses reached in her direction with its long neck and made a snorting noise. She wasn't sure if they might bite, or if they had sharp fangs.

Inside, a tall slender woman sat before the fire. Her golden hair, streaked with white, was pulled back into a coiled bun. She had the long, thin features common among the townspeople.

"Are you ready?" the woman asked, looking up.

"Yes, we are," Terni told her. "Mia, this is my sister Danli. She has agreed to take you into her care. You'll be leaving with her in the morning."

"But I don't want to leave here!" Mia protested. "I like it here!"

"I'm sorry, dear. But I did tell you that we could only keep you for a few days, so we sent a messenger Danli's way. Now let's make supper."

∞∞∞

Early the following morning after Mia woke up, she ate porridge and eggs, dressed, and packed a few small food items in a bag Terni provided, as she had no possessions of her own left. As Mia said a somber goodbye and went outside where Danli waited, sheer mists shrouded the gray and brown trunks of the trees. The sky was overcast again, diffusing soft muted light everywhere. The red and gold leaves began to rain more heavily from the trees, floating down in zigzagged arcs. Danli had the horses ready with saddles.

"You've never ridden a horse before, have you?" Danli asked in a voice huskier than Terni's.

"No."

"Let me show you how to mount the saddle." Danli demonstrated, putting one of her booted feet in a stirrup and then grasping the saddle to pull her weight up and throw her other leg over the horse, gracefully in spite of the long gray dress she wore. She climbed back down. "Now try it. Always mount from the left. That is how we train our horses. It can spook a horse if you mount it from the right."

Because Mia was short, even getting that first foot in the stirrup was a challenge. She started to tremble as she grasped for something to hang on to. As her other foot left the ground, she fell backwards and Danli caught her. Next, Danli guided Mia's journey to the top of the saddle by supporting her rear end with her hands. Mia's dress got caught on a pack attached to the side of the horse and she struggled. When she finally got her other leg over, Danli found that the stirrups hung down too low and she adjusted the straps.

"I want to get off!" Mia cried, seeing how high up off the ground she was and how she no longer had control of her movements. The horse turned his head and took a step.

"Just relax. Just breathe," Danli urged. "You'll get used to it. This will be much faster and easier than walking. Now give his mane a scratch. It'll relax him."

"Will he bite me?"

Danli chuckled. "Not unless you make him very angry."

Cautiously, Mia reached forward and petted the back of the neck where the long white hair grew. Taking hold of the long leather reins, Danli guided her horse toward the open gate. Mia's horse started to walk, following close behind.

"This horse is moving and I didn't tell him to!" Mia exclaimed. "What if I fall off?!"

"He'll follow mine by instinct," Danli assured her. "Horses like to stay in lines. Just hold the reins, keep your feet in the stirrups, and relax."

As they left the yard and then walked down the street, Mia was still very nervous, especially as she heard dogs barking. Slowly, the regular rhythm of the horse's hooves clopping on the street began to soothe her, as the raft had when it softly glided over the ocean water in those peaceful days before the storm hit. Building the raft, floating away, the excitement of adventure, and then the trauma of being slammed underwater and nearly drowned in the violent nighttime storm—it still felt as though all of that had happened just yesterday. Mia went into a sort of trance of deep thought as Danli led the way onto the main streets, keeping to the right to let carriages pass by. The buildings thinned out and eventually they were on a dirt road leading out of the city. They strolled into the country, passing by open sheep-filled pastures and thickets of dark green pine trees. Many of the snow-capped mountain peaks rose high enough to pierce the clouds.

"Where are we going?" Mia asked as the horses walked down a quiet road.

"I live on a homestead near the mountains. I raise sheep and goats."

"How long will I be staying there?"

"If your parents are, erm, not found, and no one else decides to take you in, I may simply keep you in my care. I'll try to avoid putting you in an orphanage. Those places are horrid."

"Are they looking for my parents, like they said they would?" Mia asked.

"Yes. It will take the ship a while to go out to that island. But when they return, the news will reach us."

"Why couldn't I stay at Terni's house?"

"Her husband dislikes children; they make him uncomfortable. They were keeping you for a few days out of kindness, but he did not want a child around longer than that."

"Do they not have children of their own?" Mia asked, a little annoyed and offended. "And I'm getting older. I'm not a small toddler anymore."

"I know. You are almost a little lady, but he is mostly comfortable around grownups. To answer your question, they did not wish to have children. But some years ago, my sister fell pregnant unexpectedly. I took the little girl, Cady, into my care. She is eleven years old now. I think you'll enjoy her companionship."

"So this Cady lives with you? Do you have other children around?"

"I have one surviving son, Nel. He is fifteen years old."

"He's close to the same age as my brother." Mia's heart sank at the thought of living with another teenage boy. What if he had the same aggressive inclinations as Deto?

"Nel is a good boy who keeps to himself. He's a very quiet sort. He was a chatterbox when he was very small, but he grew quiet when he lost his brother."

"What happened to him?"

"My oldest was sent to battle about a decade ago, after we were wracked with a terrible plague that spread through the west. Dakoris didn't get hit as hard as some of the other countries, but oh, it was still terrible."

"It was a disease?"

"Yes. A hideous disease."

"Did your son catch it?"

"No, he was fortunate enough not to. A country in the east called Kai'Zi sent the plague here to try to wipe out the west."

"Really? That's a terrible thing to do!"

"Yes, it was horrid. Understandably, the countries of the west were very angry. Each one raised an army, with a little help from some of the eastern nations as well. A country to the north of us also built mechanical soldiers. Quite a brilliant invention, but not enough without the human armies. My son was killed in battle."

"Oh, no. How old was he?"

"Seventeen. He was going to marry a girl down the road as soon as he got back, too. She went on to marry another young man and they have a family now. But I think she still misses him. And I miss him every day as well."

"That's horrible, that he died young. I'm sorry."

The day was starting to warm up, but only slightly. The cloud cover cast a dreary pall over their surroundings. They stopped at a small town where the houses were made out of wooden logs. Danli helped Mia out of her saddle, hitched the horses, and led her inside a tavern. Noisy cloaked men sat at a bar, tossing their heads back and gulping from ceramic mugs. A bartender poured yellow liquid from wooden ale kegs into the mugs. Danli and Mia seated themselves at a round table. Danli asked a woman for two bowls of goat stew with cups of goat's milk and handed her a small fistful of bronze coins of varying sizes. It started to seem as though every meal in Dakoris was derived from goats. Despite this country's monotonous diet, the portions were still generous enough to make Mia happy after growing up hungry.

"You don't dye your hair?" Mia asked Danli as they ate, noting her graying blond tresses.

"No, it's something that the city folks tend to do. They are more concerned about appearances. I used to dye my hair, and then I no longer saw the point. My husband left me and I felt no desire to attract another man. I still have a stockpile of old dye ingredients you may use."

Mia told Danli the story about getting spat on by an old man the other day, learning that she resembled some race that people hated, and how it led to her own newly red hair.

"I'm sure that your hair is simply sun-bleached from living on that island your whole life," said Danli. "People of other races are occasionally born with that very pale or silver hair, but it was a trademark of the Kai'Zi people. The ones who sent the plague."

"Maybe that man thought I was one of them?" Mia asked. It made a bit more sense to her now why her hair color could evoke such a strong reaction, after the despicable thing that group of people had done.

"Or at least reminded him of them. The Kai'Zi, as far as I know, have been killed off in the war, or pretty close. Not everyone will think you have anything to do with them, but you'll certainly want to keep dyeing your hair to be safe, since some folks don't think things through and will give you a hard time. You'll need to cover the roots every few weeks or so."

After eating, Danli gave handfuls of hay to the horses and led them to a stream where they bent their long graceful necks down for a drink. Danli and Mia got back on the saddles and continued on their journey. They went up in elevation, climbing trails on rocky foothills. The air got colder the higher they went, and Danli warned Mia to rest as much as she could the first week or so at her new home to avoid getting something called mountain sickness. That night, Danli led the horses into a tiny town and they stayed at an inn consisting of three rooms. The next day was also spent riding.

It was evening and the gray sky was beginning to darken by the time they reached Danli's property, nestled on a slope and edged with dark green pine and fir trees. Sheep and goats roamed around on the brown grass, making braying noises. A tall, rail-thin boy threw hay out for the animals and tilted a bucket to fill their water troughs.

"Hi, Nel," Danli called. Her son only nodded in response, not smiling. He had a long face underneath his wavy reddish-gold hair.

As Danli nudged the horses into a stable, a white-and-gray monster raced across the grass, making shrill yipping noises and coming straight at Mia. She screamed and dashed into a nearby unused stable, slamming the low door.

"What's got you so frightened?" Danli asked as the monster scratched at the outside of the door and whined. "It's just my shepherd dog, Josi. She wants to say hello." To Mia's horror, the woman swung the door wide open and allowed the dog into the stable. With its fanged jaws open, the dog charged straight at Mia, who was cornered. She froze in blind terror as the thing jumped on her and attacked, claws flailing against her. She closed her eyes and made peace with the fact that these were her last moments. After surviving the storm that broke the raft and nearly drowned her, now she was going to get mauled to pieces thanks to this cruel woman.

Mia opened her eyes when the pain never came. The dog wasn't tearing her flesh from her bones. Instead, it was licking her with a long, pink tongue! The dog's bushy tail whipped from side to side.

"Go on," Danli encouraged. "Scratch her behind her ears. There's nothing to fear."

A tremor still made Mia's hand shake violently as she reached up. Basking in the attention, the fuzzy long-snouted dog tilted her head for more petting, and then rolled over onto her back for a belly rub. Mia started to laugh at herself.

Danli's house was a multi-room log cabin, similar to most other buildings Mia had seen for the past day. They went inside with Danli's silent son and the excited dog. Terni's daughter Cady, the girl Danli was raising, sat on a rug in front of the stone fireplace, bathed in the warm orange glow. Long straight, honey-gold hair hung over the back of her wool cloak. She looked up shyly with a freckled face when Danli introduced Mia. The small crowd gathered for a dinner of cabbage and goat roast that had been simmering over the fire, muttering the routine prayer to the sheep-goddess. The dog gnawed on soup bones as she rested on the wooden floor underneath the table.

When bedtime came, Mia was given a few cloth-wrapped hot stones to warm her bed and shown to the room she would share with Cady. The two beds rested against opposite walls, covered with the now-familiar woven wool blankets. Between the beds, an open trunk overflowed with toys: dolls, blocks, and wooden puzzles. Mia smiled at the sight of that and the shelf filled with books she couldn't wait to read.

After Danli left Cady and Mia alone together, both felt too bashful to say much.

"Have a good night," Cady finally whispered before putting out the oil lamp on the nightstand.

"Have a good night," Mia returned the blessing.

Outside the window, the clouds had parted, exposing the stars, moon, and white arch that was noticeably smaller than the one Mia had grown up with. It still took up a good portion of the sky. Faint celestial light came through the window, creating squares on the floor. Things rustled outside, and far off in the distance, strange drawn-out howls echoed through the trees. Though Mia had never heard those plaintive, haunting sounds before, they sounded somehow familiar.

"What is that?" Mia whispered.

"What's what?" Cady said from the other bed, groggy.

"Whatever is making those funny noises outside."

"Those are wolves."

"Are they monsters?"

"No. They're animals with pointy ears that look sort of like dogs."

"Will they hurt us?"

"No, but every once in a while, they eat one of the sheep or goats. They eat the neighbors' chickens, too."

"Won't they eat us too?"

"No. They're frightened of us; don't worry. We should get some sleep."

The more howls Mia heard, the more a strange longing welled up inside her. She got the urge to run outdoors in the night and feel the thrill and freedom of wind whipping through her hair. Despite this temptation that suddenly came on, Mia did not want to get in trouble with Danli, and knew that the best thing to do right now, in this new house with these people she hardly knew, was to stay put.

Mia had trouble relaxing enough to fall asleep. Once the howls of the wolves outside died down, she kept thinking uneasily about the boy in the next room, waiting for the door to the bedroom to creak open or for her to be caught by surprise in her sleep as he yanked her dress off. Once she finally drifted off, though, she slept undisturbed.

∞∞∞

In the morning, Mia awoke feeling terrible, as hot as she had while floating and sunburned out on the ocean. Her muscles ached and creaked and virtually screamed with every movement. She crawled out of her bed, bare feet landing on the chilly wood floor, and shuffled in her white nightgown toward the mirror that hung on the wall. To her horror, her cheeks were encrusted with angry red sores. Throwing her slender hands upward and seeing them covered in spots as well, Mia gasped and backed away from the mirror. She had the plague! She was going to die!

Cady writhed in her bed, turned over, yawned, and opened and rubbed her eyes, which went wide when they landed on Mia nearby.

"Aunt Danli! Aunt Danli!" Cady called, jumping out of bed and running to the kitchen. "Mia has the red pox!"

Quickly, Danli came to examine Mia, ordering her to get back in bed and laying a hand on her forehead. "My goodness, you're burning up. Cady, go fetch me a sick bucket."

Cady brought a pail to the bedside just in time for Mia's stomach to begin turning violently.

"Do... I... have the plague?" Mia mumbled, wiping her mouth after a fit of sickness. "Am... I... going to die?"

"No, no, it's not that."

"Are you sure?!"

"Yes, I'm sure. If you had the plague, your insides would turn to liquid and you would bleed from every opening on your body. You have the red pox, a disease most children get. You'll be miserable for a while, but you should live."

"Does anyone... still... get the plague?"

"Not often. A very brilliant healer found a cure for it. I'm so happy it's behind us. Now try not to worry and get some rest. You'll be confined to bed for a few days."

It was a bad day. Mia couldn't keep any food down, and only crawled out of her bed to use the chamberpot stored under it. Periodically, Danli brought cups of bitter hot medicine and ordered her to drink them.

"I'm sorry I'm burdening you," Mia apologized, feeling terrible guilt for needing to be babied, as Danli brought her another cup of bad-tasting boiled herbs in the evening after taking the sick bucket and chamberpot outside to empty.

"Burdening me? How so?" Danli lit the oil lamp on the nightstand.

"By being sick, and you having to take care of me and clean up after me."

"Everyone knows that children get sick sometimes."

"When I was still living on the island, my parents would get cross with me when I got hurt or didn't feel well. They would leave me by myself. They would call me a burden."

"It sounds as if they were rather cruel."

"I didn't like them sometimes. The one I liked most was my eldest sister. When I was small, she would sing to me, tell me stories, teach me to read, and act as though she was my mother. They said it was my fault when she broke her leg and got sick and died, even though I wasn't there when she fell. Sometimes I wonder though... whether that really was my fault."

Mia still remembered that horrible day when she was six, hearing the screams from far off, and then running back to camp to find her sister lying on the ground crying, her leg wrapped in bloody dirty cloth at the place where the bone pierced the flesh of her thigh. A couple of days later, Lata looked awful, sweat-beaded and delirious with fever, mumbling incoherently by the time she took her last breath.

"It wasn't your fault," Danli reassured her. Those words were like water in a desert to Mia. "Your parents were grief-stricken and lashing out, but it doesn't make it right to place the blame on you."

"But now I just feel terrible that I didn't take them with me, or didn't come back for them, and then that volcano erupted."

"Mia, don't trouble yourself so much thinking about your regrets. It would have been difficult to make a raft large enough for five people with your bare hands. And your family would have been rescued afterwards, had they been found. They still might be; a ship is on the hunt for them right now. We're still not sure that the island that erupted is the same one you grew up on."

"I'm going to be sick." Mia leaned over the bucket.

"I'll mix up more medicine for when you can keep it down, hopefully by tomorrow," said Danli. When Mia was finished throwing up, Danli laid a cool moist cloth over her roasting forehead.

In Mia's fever dreams that night, she found herself back on the island with its wide open bright blue sky and fine-grained sugarlike beaches. The breeze carried the familiar sweet scent of tropical flowers. Whether or not the island still existed as Mia remembered it, she carried every inch of its contours in her mind, every nook and cranny. She looked everywhere for her parents and brother and snooty surviving sister, and they were nowhere to be found. Their campfire still smoldered near the western beach. And then wolves howled deep in the palm trees. The sad-sounding howls drew closer, but the wolves stayed invisible. Driven by the desire to see the animals, Mia searched and searched for them as well as her family.

When Mia awoke in the morning, her skin itched horribly. She scratched at the crusty sores on her arms until they bled.

"Don't do that!" Cady warned from the other bed. "You'll get scars for the rest of your life!"

"But the itching... it's just... awful!" Mia growled, curling her fingers and gritting her teeth.

Danli came in to check on Mia. When she complained of the maddening need to scratch, Danli decided that it was time to put together a soothing skin poultice. Before applying it, Mia needed to bathe. After drawing buckets of water from the well, heating them over the fire, and pouring them into a large tub in the next room, Danli pulled Mia out of the bed and led her to the tub. After she was left alone with soap and herbs to scrub herself with, Mia let her nightgown fall to the floor and stepped into the warm, soothing water. Rays of soft morning sunlight tumbled in from the window above. Mia wiped away the sweat that had gathered on her pale, red-dotted skin from the fever. Fortunately, the need to vomit was gone for now, though Mia had no appetite.

Danli knocked and came in. Mia, still crouched in the tub, looked up.

"Are you done scrubbing?" Danli asked. "I'll need to dry you and put on the medicine."

Mia stood up as Danli gently patted her dry with a rag. As Danli dried her back from behind, she suddenly dropped the rag and stepped backward, breathing in sharply.

"Is everything all right?" Mia finally asked.

"Uh... yes. Yes, everything is... fine." Stumbling over her words, Danli picked the rag back up and finished drying Mia. She was completely silent as she scooped gobs of thick warm herbal mixture in her fingers and smeared it on the sores. It instantly cooled them down and relieved the unbearable itching.

"I've gotten the spots that are hard to reach," Danli said at last, her voice unusually strained and detached, her expression pale and visibly shaken. "You're old enough to get the rest of them yourself. Just put a few dabs on each sore. When it dries, put your nightgown back on and return to bed." She turned and curtly left the room.

After climbing back into bed, Mia had to wait a long time for Danli to come with her cups of medicine. Something seemed wrong; Danli was too quiet, looking flustered and biting her lip. But when the last of the medicine arrived at bedtime, Danli acted more at ease.

It took five days for Mia to fully recover from the red pox. And even after the sores nearly disappeared from her pale skin, Mia was warned to not go outside or overextend herself for a while. She amused herself with Cady's books, and learned very quickly how to solve her wooden puzzles. Cady taught Mia to build houses from her bright painted blocks. Cady remained patient, despite Mia's awkward, possessive style of play. When piecing together a puzzle, she didn't want anyone else touching it, too accustomed to hoarding and protecting her treasures from her family. She also cried easily when her feelings got bruised or someone removed a cherished toy or book from her sight. When Cady got frustrated with Mia, Danli reminded her what Mia had been through—she'd grown up in isolation, with no children her age to play with, and then lost her things and possibly her family.

Weeks after the red pox passed, Terni came to visit her sister, and to see how Mia was settling in. As soon as Terni came through the front door, Mia jumped up from her spot in front of the fire and threw her arms around the woman's waist. They chattered for a bit.

After dinner, Danli sent Cady and Nel out to the stable

to do chores. Once they were gone, Danli grasped Terni's long skinny arm and softly asked, "May I have a word with you? In private?"

Terni nodded and the two sisters stepped outside through the front door in their wool cloaks.

Mia sat alone in front of the fire, anxious that she had no idea what her two favorite women, her stand-in mothers, were discussing outside. When Mia's curiosity got the best of her, she dared to sneak out the door. The cold night air numbed her cheeks a bit. She crept along using the silent footstep she'd taught herself during those breezy tropical island nights, following the faint sound of their voices. They were just around the corner of a storage hut, draped deep in shadow. Mia flattened against the trunk of a pine tree, also hiding in the shadows, and listened in.

"I still say it's not possible," Terni insisted. "If it's true, then what on earth would she be doing on a desert island?"

"Like I was saying, I could only think of one possibility, but I cannot imagine how it would work."

"Are you absolutely sure that's what you saw?"

"I thought it was unmistakable. But now I wonder if my eyes have fooled me. It makes no sense."

"Just behave like everything is normal," said Terni. "Keep the mark hidden if it's there and keep her hair dyed. She could be hiding something, but she really doesn't seem to know any more than we do."

"You promise to tell no one?"

"You have my word."

"I hear my son coming," said Danli as footsteps crunched across the dry grass. "Hello, Nel. Let's get Cady and come inside."

Mia crept soundlessly back in, keeping to the shadows, and was sitting inconspicuously before the fire, petting the dog as she laid her head on her lap, when the rest returned. Without showing any signs of what was on her mind, she silently turned the strange conversation over and over, knowing it was about her. That was all she could understand. The rest—something about a mark—remained a mystery. Somehow she knew that she shouldn't ask questions about these things, lest she get in trouble for eavesdropping. She burned all over with excruciating curiosity.

A couple of days later, Terni set out to leave. First, she hugged her sister, her daughter Cady, and her nephew who looked down and stiffened at her touch. And then she quickly put her arms around Mia. "It was nice seeing you again," she said. "I'll be back soon for another visit. And the rescue mission will be back from the ocean soon with the results of their search."

Mia stared out the window, wide-eyed and forlorn, as Terni's horse trotted off down the rocky mountain road toward the coast. Once she was well out of sight and breakfast was finished, Danli sent Cady and Nel outside to do chores and began to scrub her dishes clean. Mia was again left alone, and the conversation she'd overhead last night stayed perpetually on her mind. She remembered the second day of the full-blown red pox, when Danli had gasped and dropped the cloth when patting Mia's bare back dry. And then in their frantic covert discussion outside in the darkness, Danli and her sister said something about a mark.

Mia went into her empty bedroom and shut the door. She stood with her back to the mirror on the wall and turned her head to look over her shoulder. She pulled up her floor-length dress, bunching up the fabric in her hands until her lower back showed.

A small silvery white design, almost like a scar, graced the china-white skin above her underpants. Multiple equal arms radiated out from a center with intricate little lines in between. Mia never knew she had this. Was she born with it? Or was it a scar or brand of some sort? She remembered no injury that could have caused the mark, and it looked too fine and symmetrical to be from an accident. When her parents beat her with sticks or a whip, they usually aimed for the upper back. And though the strikes had sometimes left bruises, they generally did not leave scars.

Though it didn't seem likely, maybe the mark came from some particularly severe beating Mia had either blocked out or was too young to remember. As she looked back on the corporal punishments, Mia grew angry. Mother and Father had never physically disciplined her siblings, no matter how naughty they'd been. Instead, they spoiled them as much as a parent could spoil a child while stranded on an island. Lata, Sireh, and Deto got jewels from Father's collection for their birthdays, and they took first priority during meals. Only Mia had suffered the bare-back punishments, face pressed up against the trunk of the palm tree with her wrists bound on the other side.

Danli walked into the bedroom to find Mia sitting on her bed, head in hands, crying.

"What's wrong, child?" she asked.

"My parents... they... hated me," Mia sniffled. "They liked Sireh and Deto, and Lata before she died. And they hated me."

"I'm sure that they did not hate you," Danli reassured. "You're having a lot of emotions going in all directions. They were in a hard situation and probably acting in ways they wouldn't otherwise."

After Mia managed to stop her tears, Danli decided to have her help wash dishes and cook a meal of porridge. As Mia scrubbed the dishes in a basin with cloth and the same herbal soap she used during her baths, Danli began to ask about her family. "What did they look like? Hair, eyes, features?"

"Well, they all had sort of big noses and round cheeks and thin lips and big eyes. They all had brown hair except me. Father and Deto had straight hair, like me, and Mother and my sisters had curly hair."

"What about their eye color?"

"Mother and Sireh had green eyes. Father, Lata, and Deto had brown eyes. I'm the only one with blue eyes. When I saw myself in a mirror, I could see that I don't look much like them."

"Hm, it doesn't sound like it. What about their skin color?"

"Fair-skinned like we are, but tanned from being in the

sun."

"Deto and Sireh—those are odd names for a brother and sister to have. Deto's definitely a Loriar name. And I think Lata is too. But Sireh and Mia aren't. I'm not certain where those names come from."

"What's a Loriar name?" Mia asked.

"You've never heard of Loriar, have you?"

"No."

"It is a powerful country to the north. You speak in the Loriar accent, so that's probably where they came from. Come to think of it, Sireh sounds more Taniar. That is a tropical country on the border of Loriar. But unlike your family, Taniar people have dark skin and black hair. What were your parents' names?"

"Mother and Father."

"All mothers and fathers have names besides Mother and Father. What are their actual names?"

"I'm not sure. They never told me."

"That's interesting. They might not have thought it was important to tell you, since you never spoke with anyone else. About how old were your brother and sister?"

"Sireh was eighteen and Deto was sixteen. If Lata were still alive, I think she'd be about twenty."

"So they were of age and you were the youngest."

"That's true." Mia removed a ceramic cup from the soapy water. She hadn't anticipated it being so slippery with suds. It slid from her hands faster than she could react, fell to the floor, and broke into pieces. She stood frozen, looking down at the broken cup. Trembling, Mia backed slowly away. As Danli came at her, she turned into the corner of the kitchen, head sagged down and face in her hands.

"Don't be so afraid, child," Danli urged. "Come back here and help me to clean up the mess." As a cold dry hand brushed her arm, Mia flinched hard.

"What's wrong?" Danli sighed. "Why are you so afraid?"

"Please," Mia pleaded in a whisper. "If you punish me, please do it quickly."

"Punishment? You're expecting to be beaten?"

Shivering, face still deep in the corner, Mia nodded.

Much to her surprise, Danli burst out laughing. "I have many other cups like this one and can easily get a new one. Nothing worth shuddering in a corner over!"

Mia slowly turned away from the corner, still scared and meek, wide-eyed in her disbelief.

"You musn't worry about being beaten," Danli assured Mia. "That won't happen here. Now come on, relax, and help me to sweep up that broken cup."

As Mia helped with the cleanup, she couldn't believe her good fortune—that the era of painful punishments had ended, at least until she was reunited with her family—something she both looked forward to and dreaded. Mia's hands still shook as she washed and rinsed the rest of the dishes; she waited to drop another, the dish that would finally make Danli snap in her anger and get out the whip. But it never happened. Once the porridge was heating over the flames of the fire, Danli and Mia sat in the warmth and talked.

"May I ask when your birthday is?" Danli asked.

Mia thought hard. "I was born in the month of Torin. My parents never told me the day. I don't think they even knew it, because they'd been on the island a while and had sort of lost track."

"You were born on the island?"

"Yes. There was no midwife, of course. Mother said she had a much harder time with me than the others. She almost died."

Danli nodded. "I see. I wonder if the difficult birth had a part in the way she treated you? I had my first son alone because the midwife did not arrive on time and my husband was dashing about and looking for her. Her horse slipped and broke its leg. I remember being afraid and in pain, but it wasn't as bad as I'd feared. The midwife's horse wasn't as lucky. Did you know that Torin is coming right up? It's two months away. You're going to be thirteen, Mia. A little lady."

That night, Mia tossed and turned in the light from the glowing ring and full moon that streamed into the window before she fell asleep. Later, she was awakened by the panicked whimpers and thrashing of Cady in the bed across the room. Though Cady's eyes were closed, some sort of agony twisted her face. Worried, Mia slipped out of bed and gently shook Cady.

"Are you all right? Are you having a bad dream?"

Cady's eyes shot open as she screamed. "It's getting me! The darkness! It's eating me!"

"Cady! It's me, Mia!" She shook Cady's shoulder again. When Cady still did not recognize Mia in the throes of her night terror, Mia decided to bring Cady to her senses in the quickest way she knew how. Grabbing the unlit candle on the table between their beds, she rushed down the cold hallway to the fireplace, lit the wick in the coals of the fire, and then ran back to the bedroom, where Cady still struggled and moaned.

"Cady!" Mia said in a firm voice, holding up the candle to rouse her with the light. "Wake up! It's me!"

At last, Cady broke free of the bad dream, her sleepy eyes coming into focus. "It was... it was a dream," she mumbled groggily. "A monster. I..."

"Cady, there is no monster. It's me. You're safe now."

Cady flinched away from Mia and shrieked.

"Cady, what's wrong? It's okay. Everything's okay."

"Your eyes!" Cady gasped, looking up at Mia, her own eyes now huge.

"My eyes? What about my eyes?"

"Something is... wrong with them!"

"Cady, I can see perfectly fine."

"But... but... they're like an animal's! They shine!"

"What?"

Cady regained some of her composure. "Go look in the mirror, and hold that candle like you're holding it now. They shine in the darkness when there's a little bit of light!"

Skeptical, Mia crossed over and studied herself in the mirror. After cocking her head this way and that, she discovered, to her surprise, that Cady was right. If she angled her head just right, an eerie, silvery blue sheen reflected bright from her large pupils and from the mirror, which grew painful to look at. Uneasily, Mia stepped back from the mirror.

"That's funny," Mia said. "I never knew my eyes did that. Does anyone else have eyes like this?"

"Not that I know of," Cady replied, her own eyes simply glinting with moisture in the dim light from the candle flame. "Just some animals. A person's eyes should not shine like that."

"Why do animals' eyes shine, anyway?"

"So they can see better in the dark."

Mia blew out the candle and turned toward a small craft, made from yarn wrapped on sticks, which hung on the door. Even in the night, draped mostly in shadow, it stood out crisply against the grain of the wood.

"That yarn creation on the door, can you see it right now?" Mia asked Cady.

Cady sat up and strained her eyes. "No. It's too dark, even though the moon is full."

"I can see it. Maybe this is why I can sometimes do things at night without a lantern. I can see better in the dark."

"Those eyes did look spooky for a second," Cady admitted, "but now I'm a little jealous."

∞∞∞

The weather grew colder. Thicker patches of snow coated the mountains that rose like spires of rock in the south. On many days the sky was a clear, deep blue, the ring in the north as white and pure as the mountain snow. All of the leaves had fallen from the trees that weren't pines and firs, leaving them bare and gray. Bitter winds whipped through, bringing snow. Some of the storms came as small flurries; some were heavier. As the weeks went by, snow began to accumulate. The biting cold took some getting used to for Mia, but as long as she wore a thick wool cloak and linen underneath, she could tolerate the weather better than anyone had expected for a girl who grew up on a tropical island. Mia went outside to play in the snow, packing snowballs in her fingers and tossing them for the dog to chase after. On sunny days, she marveled at the brilliant sparkling of the snow, pristine under the blue and white sky. When she sat in it, getting her cloak wetter than Danli liked, and filtered the snow through her numb fingers, Mia was entranced with the way it fell softly through the air, glittering. The cold wet whiteness comforted Mia and made her feel at home. Snow looked just as she had imagined in her fantasies of the gleaming white yards outside of her dream palace, the one with the reindeer, indoor waterfalls, ice sculptures, and jade carvings.

Danli increased Mia's daily chores. She learned to feed the sheep and goats, and tend to the horses' coats and hooves. Mia was taught to spin wool into yarn with a wooden spindle.

Butchering the goats for food was the next lesson. Danli demonstrated for Mia, capturing a small horned goat, knocking him unconscious with the back of an axe to the head in a sheltered spot where snow didn't fall, and cutting his throat and waiting for the steaming blood to drain into a dark patch in the soil. It surprised Danli that spilling the blood and carving flesh did not make Mia squeamish. She'd grown up getting meat out of fish and birds and striped tarniks; she was accustomed to blood. Squeezing milk from the live goats' teats made Mia a little more nervous that the animals might bite her or kick her with their hooves.

Merchants came by from time to time to purchase wool and yarn in bulk. They often told stories of their travels. Mia and Cady ate up these tales of the outside world. Danli had friends living to the north, a married couple named Tak and Mendy with four boys, who also visited occasionally to pick up wool to pass along to merchants or just to have dinner together. The families had met through trade routes. Tak and Mendy were loud and talkative, the boys rough and obnoxious as they played outside, and they were not well-traveled and full of interesting stories like the merchants. Mia was always happy to see merchants, yet a bit relieved when these particular friends mounted their horses and wagon and left.

After accumulating money from the purchases, Danli went on solo horseback journeys to the nearest village to load her packs with whatever food and supplies she needed. She was usually back by the time the sun went down. It set earlier and earlier each day. Many evenings were devoted to reading, history, and arithmetic lessons for Nel, Cady, and Mia. Despite her limited learning opportunities on the island, it did not take Mia long to catch up. Danli also got a chance to show Mia the miracle of birth when Josi, the dog, whelped a litter of five puppies. Danli couldn't figure out how Josi became pregnant, since she was her only dog. The newborn pups were round and grayish in color, with their eyes fused shut. As the puppies' eyes and ears opened in the days that came and they began to crawl, Danli started to suspect that they were half wolf, though the idea seemed farfetched. Mia became fascinated by the wriggling little creatures as they developed a bit more each day, playing with them when Josi let her.

As Josi nursed her pups near the fire, Danli gave evening geography lessons. She unrolled an old hand-drawn map her estranged husband had left behind and taught Nel, Cady, and Mia about the cluster of countries sandwiched in the west between the polar masses of ice. To the south lay a great, impassable mountain range with glaciers and fjords. Above the southern nation of Dakoris was Parem, encompassing plains, deserts, and a large equatorial rainforest, as well as the Great Parem River featured in the childhood book that had given Mia the idea to build the raft. It amazed Mia to learn more about this legendary channel. The thick river branched out like a network of tree roots. Most known for its valuable gemstone, the Parem ruby, the country was also the home of the healer who had found a treatment for the lethal plague with his rabbit's blood tonic after he learned that furriers in the southern plains, who ate a lot of rabbit meat, never caught the horrid disease.

Loriar, a world superpower and probably the original land of Mia's heritage, took up much of the north. Many of the people in this heavily forested country made a living by raising cattle and selling their milk and meat. Logging and gold mining kept their economy turning.

Along with the desert of northern Parem, edging the southern border of Loriar was the rather narrow country of Taniar. People often traveled to its warm climate of pink-sand beaches and palm trees for recreational purposes. Foreigners from Parem or Dakoris moved there for the health benefits of its temperate climate. The natives lived on a coconut-based diet and many made a living farming tropical fruits or cannabis. Life in Taniar sounded too much like Mia's imprisonment on the island, and she had difficulty understanding why people would want to go to such a place for fun.

When Mia asked where the island of her birth was, Danli couldn't be sure, since not all of the islands in the world had been studied or mapped by the sea explorers. But she had a pretty good guess. She pointed just south of the equator in the middle of the blue Dorov Ocean.

Cady inquired about the eastern countries, but Danli didn't have any maps of those. She did not feel it was necessary to waste time studying the other side of the world. Since the war between the west and Kai'Zi, very few people traveled between the western and eastern nations, except to one country with rumors of an active slave trade.

∞∞∞

The snowy weather dragged on. As Mia's thirteenth birthday drew close, she still engaged in child's play, but her height shot up almost overnight. She needed new dresses as the old ones quickly got too short and small, and she developed a ravenous appetite. Her hips widened, and the growing lumps on her chest alarmed her.

Nel, Danli's surviving son, was as quiet and withdrawn as ever. Every night, Mia had trouble falling asleep, waiting for her dress to be yanked off her body as soon as she drifted off. But the teenager hardly looked at her, never entered her and Cady's shared bedroom, and acted as though she was not there. Gradually Mia's fear of the boy faded. The chorus of the wolves howling somewhere far off in the white landscape outside, one of them possibly the father of Josi's puppies, soothed her to sleep.

Mia got to know Cady better through their daytime play and bedtime talks, and mirrored her behavior. The two girls became best friends. Cady confided in Mia that she secretly liked Thom, an adolescent boy who lived down the road, and that when she got big enough to leave this place she wanted to study to be a healer. And hopefully, get married to Thom and have lots of babies, too.

Mia, perfectly content with where she had ended up, could see herself raising sheep for the rest of her life. She told Cady that, as well as a lot of stories about her past. Having never seen a tropical island or coconut palm, Cady took in the stories with great interest. But in spite of their deepening friendship, Mia stopped just short of telling Cady about the unusual mark on her lower back that Danli wanted kept hidden, and the conversation she'd overhead between Danli and her sister. A nagging voice in Mia's head told her to be careful; she didn't know what it meant but it was something not good.

One day, Mia and Cady finished their chores well before the sun went down, so they decided to take a walk down the road and say hello to Thom, the boy Cady liked, and ask if he wanted to keep one of Josi's puppies after they were weaned. The puppy offer, Cady admitted to Mia, was mostly just an excuse to talk to Thom. The last two times they'd tried to visit him, his parents told the girls he was busy doing chores in the fields. Now, Cady worked up the nerve to try a third time. They closed the wooden gate of Danli's property behind them. Their boots crunched through the beaten-down crust of snow on the damp, muddy road. Slushy snow fell from the deep green pine boughs above their heads, surprising Mia when it slid down the back of her dress and ice-cold water trickled unpleasantly over her body.

Something rustled in a nearby thicket of trees. It was Thom, who aimed up at tree boughs with his slingshot and shot down snow with pebbles. Cady waved shyly as Thom turned around. Mia could see why Cady had such a crush on him; his wispy reddish hair framed finely built, handsome features.

"Uh, Thom," Cady began awkwardly. "My dog, uh, she had puppies. The puppies are close to being weaned. Would you... like to bring one home?"

"I'd like a puppy, but I would have to ask my ma and pa. They already have a shepherd dog for the farm. I'll let you know what they say."

"Okay. Uh... hope they let you take a puppy. They are quite precious."

"Cady, would you and... I'm sorry, what's your name?" Thom looked at Mia for the first time.

"Mia."

"Would you like to try my slingshot? It belonged to my pa when he was a boy."

"Sure," said Mia, curious. She had never used a slingshot before, and Thom quickly showed her how.

After a few tries with a handful of pebbles, Mia shot a branch thick with snow and watched it rain down. She turned around to find Thom and Cady gone. They'd left without warning, leaving nothing but footprints behind. Burning with a left-out, hurt, forgotten feeling, Mia set off to look for them. She stomped down the trail of footprints.

Mia stopped when her skin suddenly crawled with a sense of being watched. Slowly, cautiously, Mia turned around, peeking through the thick red-brown trunks of the pine trees. Out of the corner of her eye, a quick shadow rushed across the snow. As she tiptoed toward it, she heard rustling. Something, or someone, hid in the foliage. Cold with fear, Mia turned back and ran in the opposite direction.

"Cady!" Mia called, frightened as footsteps fell audibly behind her. Knowing she was being chased, she rushed as fast as she could. Slipping on ice packed beneath the snow, Mia fell face-first. And then she got up, brushed the cold snow from her face and stinging palms, and ran again.

"Mia, what's wrong?" Cady asked, suddenly appearing with Thom. They held hands, their fingers interlaced underneath the generous sleeves of their long cloaks.

"Somebody's... chasing... me," Mia puffed out.

The three of them stopped talking to listen. Again, something shook in the trees, and then a horse's hooves thundered down the road. All of them held their breath until the hoofbeats faded.

"That's so odd," Cady observed. "It seemed like someone was there, getting closer, and now they just ran away. I wonder who that could have been?"

"I've got to get home," Thom told them, apologetic, after he looked at the angle of the sun and the lengthening shadows. "My ma and pa are expecting me back before supper."

Mia and Cady also set out on the way home. Fresh hoofprints, now small lakes filling with muddy water, ran the length of the road. Mia wanted to follow them, but they extended well past Danli's home. Cady pulled Mia back through the gate, insisting on not being out too late.

For weeks afterward, whenever she was outside doing chores or playing, Mia struggled with an uneasy sensation of being watched. But whenever she turned, there was nothing out of place. Cady repeatedly reassured her that no one lurked in the shadows.

∞ ∞ ∞

For Mia's thirteenth birthday, Danli and Cady surprised her with a basket of chocolate and dried fruit treats to celebrate. As far as Mia could recall, until now, nobody had ever done anything nice for her just because of growing a year older.

A couple of days after Mia received the treats, two mounted men came to the gate. Danli peeked out the windows and asked Nel, Cady, and Mia to go to their bedrooms and shut the doors. As Cady and Mia sat on their beds in a nervous silence, Danli let the men through the gate, and then into the house after they hitched their horses. Mia listened to the heavy footsteps of the men entering the house and their hushed voices as they talked with Danli. Mia heard mention of her name. Danli came and gently knocked on the bedroom door.

"Mia," she whispered, "these men are here to speak with you."

Worried she was in some kind of trouble, Mia reluctantly stepped out to the main area of the house, her heart practically jumping up to her throat. One man was military, wearing a chain mail shirt and tall strapped boots, sword hanging in a sheath from a belt at his hips. Next to him was another unfamiliar man dressed in a plain cloak. Their expressions were grave. Mia had trouble meeting their eyes. She looked down, her dyed red hair falling in strings over her pale face.

"Mia," said the cloaked man, "as you'll recall, you were rescued from the Dorov Ocean. You stated that you had come from an island, where your parents and brother and sister lived. Shortly after you left the island, a volcanic eruption took place in the area. A rescue mission was sent out to search for your family."

"Did they find them?" Mia asked, frantic and hoping for positive news. "Are they okay?"

"Our ship traveled to every island we could find in the area. We checked the volcano. That entire island was scorched in the eruption, and lava was still draining into the ocean. The other islands were small and uninhabited. I'm very sorry, Mia."

"My family wasn't found?"

"No. We believe that your family perished in the eruption. Again, we're sorry to be bringing you this tragic news."

After the two men left, Mia burrowed into her bed, hot

tears trickling down her face. She seesawed from one emotion to another, from disbelief to devastation. Danli brought Mia a cup of hot tea, and Cady stroked her shoulder. Neither really knew what to say. Josi, the dog, laid on top of Mia, licking her face in attempt to comfort her. Jari, the fuzzy silver puppy they had decided to keep, followed suit.

"Aunt Danli, are you going to send Mia to an orphanage now?" Cady asked, a note of panic rising in her voice.

"No, I'm not," Danli reassured Cady. "After all of the upheaval in her life, I cannot, in good conscience, put her in a place where she knows no one, where she'll be lonely and possibly never find family until she's married. She knows us. She's comfortable here."

Even with the confidence that she wouldn't be cast into an orphanage, Mia withdrew into a storm of sadness and confusion for days. It became difficult for her to get up, to do chores, and even to eat. She spoke to Cady about her feelings at bedtime, venting the grief and her guilt that clouded her thoughts. Now that she was officially an orphan, left with no surviving parents or siblings, Mia knew she'd never be the same. All she'd ever wanted was to make her family happy. And then she selfishly left on that raft in the night, abandoning them to a certain death. Despite all the reassurance to the contrary from Danli and Cady, who were confident that she never meant for her family to die, Mia felt like a monster, even a killer. It only amplified the remorse she had carried for years, questioning whether her parents were right when they blamed her for her oldest sister's death.

If Mia had found a way to rescue her family, to build rafts big enough for them all, would they be living together much more happily now, her parents kinder, her remaining sister smiling at and speaking to her, her brother leaving her in peace? Mia would never know.

∞ ∞ ∞

The winter terminally wore on, with long hours of darkness. The winds blew and blew, carrying thick storms of snow, and Mia almost forgot what warm weather felt like. She, Danli, Cady, and Nel chopped firewood, relying on the fire and the warm stones in their beds to not freeze. Mia tried to keep her mind off the deaths of her family members with books and games and her chores. The long periods of darkness often matched the moods Mia kept hidden inside.

They all started to grow weary of winter, even as midwinter passed and they celebrated the solstice holiday with a big feast of pork and preserved fruit. Danli's friends Tak and Mendy and their four boys, along with Cady's crush Thom and his family from down the road, came over to share in the food, making for a big, noisy gathering. After the festivities, the sun started to shine for longer periods. As the snow at last began to thin and melt away, green grass poked through the white crusts, and pale green leaves and flowers emerged from some of the trees. Even as spring turned into full, green summer, with lush knee-deep wildflower-dotted grass and icy babbling brooks from the snowmelt off the mountaintops, the weather wasn't as warm as what Mia remembered on the island. Nights still held a chill, even though the summer sky was not dark for as long as it had been on the island.

One midsummer day, Mia and Cady were outside, playing tag and hide-and-go-seek, while Nel and Danli had left for the afternoon to shop for supplies. The neighbor boy Thom had come over to join the girls in their games, and the three of them raced around in the grassy flowered pasture, which was coated with golden sunlight. Josi the dog eventually ran over to play, and Mia turned her attention away from the lackadaisical game of tag. After overcoming her fear of dogs when she had first arrived in Dakoris in the fall, Mia now enjoyed Josi's style of roughhousing. She crouched down and the dog charged at her, teeth bared, and gently gnawed at her arms and hands in a mock attack.

Mia, on all fours, played make-believe that she was a furry

dog too, growling and pretending that her hands were paws, her teeth fangs. Her imaginary form began to seem so real that she was almost certain she had shrunk. Smells Mia had not noticed before hit her nose pungently. The moist blades of grass combined with the soil to create an earthy aroma, and the ammonia of urine from the nearby goat pen slammed into Mia like a rock.

Something startled Josi, who jumped away from Mia in fear. The dog crabwalked backwards, tail lowered and eyes wide. When Mia looked up, Thom and Cady also backed away, their hands clapped over their mouths.

Confused as to what went wrong, Mia backed away too, and then closed her eyes and cowered. Something was wrong with her arms and legs too; they felt awkward, the proportions all wrong, and she nearly tripped. Finally, she stood up, brushed her hair out of her face, and opened her eyes. The world stopped stinking so much. Cady and Thom still stared at Mia, their faces pale.

"What's wrong, you two?" Mia asked. "You look like you've seen a ghost."

"You... you... how did you do that?" Thom stammered.

"Do what?"

"You turned into a wolf!" Cady cried.

"Wait... a wolf? This is a joke, isn't it?"

"I saw it too!" Thom insisted. "All of a sudden, there was this whitish-silver wolf standing there in your place."

"And then the wolf disappeared, and you were standing there again, right where it was," Cady added. "Right where you are now." She lifted a slender hand to point at the base of Mia's dress. Her finger trembled weakly.

"That's ridiculous! No one turns into a wolf."

"I don't have the slightest idea how it happened, but I know what I saw. And Thom, you're sure you saw it too?"

"Indeed, I saw it," Thom agreed. "Don't know how to explain it, but it happened right before my eyes!"

"Are you sure you two aren't joking?" Mia asked.

"No, we're not joking." Their expressions were grave.

"It's impossible," Mia insisted. "Like something out of a fairy story. Those things can't really happen. But... I did feel funny." Mia's senses had changed. She didn't want to believe what they were telling her. It sounded like something parents would tell very small children, or a magical event that would occur in a book—but had she not smelled things she couldn't smell before?

"Could it be witchery?" Thom postulated. "I don't know much about witchery, but my pa has said a few things about witches, that some of them can change shape."

"I don't think so." Cady shook her head. "I don't think witches are real. Mia is not a witch."

"I didn't even mean to do that, whatever it was that happened," Mia explained. "I didn't expect it."

After some more tense conversation, Mia, Cady, and Thom still could not explain what had happened, but they agreed to keep quiet about it with others, at least until Mia herself had a glimmer of understanding as to that day's bizarre event. Cady and Thom had no intention of telling grownups anyway. Who would even believe them?

Mia's life had already been far too confusing, and now something that much more inexplicable had just happened. Her head raced with anxious thoughts for the rest of the day, and she was distant, not saying much, during supper and at bedtime. After Cady fell asleep, Mia still tossed and turned in her bed, thinking about the strange event earlier. Finally, she got up and tiptoed out of the room, hoping to clear her head.

Barefoot, Mia stepped outside onto the cool grass, where the nearly full moon and the ring turned the rugged mountainous landscape silver. She stalked off into the woods, climbing over the fence that bound the property. A cool, refreshing breeze rushed past, making the trees quake. Closing her eyes, Mia tried to bring back the sensations of earlier, when she had been playing with Josi the dog. She wanted to see if she could change forms again at will, or if it was beyond her control.

She crouched down and soon discovered that she could, in fact, change on demand. Her hands and feet turned into padded paws, and smells became stronger again, almost unbearable. Her clothing vanished; where it went, she did not know. Growing accustomed to walking in her new form, Mia zigzagged from place to place, sniffing scents she'd never known before. New sounds also came to her ears from far off. Danli's goats made startled sounds from their pens several yards across the fence, sensing a predator in the trees.

Once she gained more stability, Mia broke into a run, loping gracefully along. Running came naturally, more thrilling than ever before in her gangly two-legged human body. The grass rushed fast underneath her, turning into a blur, as the breeze whipped exhilaratingly through her fur. Before getting too carried away or allowing herself to stray too far, Mia returned to the privacy of the trees, changed back, and then walked back to the house and went to bed. Cady did not stir.

Mia began to sneak out at night on a regular basis to explore life in this other form. She never told Danli or even Cady, as the two girls drifted apart after Cady's shock at seeing Mia's unexplained shapeshifting ability. Though Cady held to the agreement to keep it a secret, her treatment of Mia subtly changed; as if she'd become more of a curiosity and less of a person. Cady stopped telling Mia her secrets and stopped sharing her excitement over her crush on the neighbors' boy.

Occasionally during the nights, Mia saw other wolves far off in the trees or standing proudly on outcroppings of rock, including a large male who looked suspiciously like Josi's now mostly-grown puppies. They answered her when she threw her head back and howled, but never came closer.

In this form, Mia was overtaken with the impulse to hunt —to taste raw flesh. Sometimes she even ate strips from dead fly-ridden animals she sniffed out on the ground, things she'd never dream of touching at the dinner table when in the form of a girl.

One autumn night, Mia made the mistake of exploring too close to Thom's family's farm, caught up in the excitement of the sounds and scents. Tonight, the sleeping sheep just looked so delectable. Though Mia always held back the temptation to chase and take down live animals, especially someone's sacred pets, her stomach rumbled. A twig snapped underneath her paw, startling the sheep, who began to bleat loudly. Thom's gray-haired, bearded father came outside in his night clothes, carrying an oil lamp and a cudgel. Mia turned to run away but it was too late—he caught a glimpse of the wolf. Thom's father raced angrily across the property as Mia got out of sight.

After this close call, Mia was badly shaken and had difficulty sleeping after returning to her bed.

A couple of days later, Danli encountered Thom's father in the road and stopped to chat. He complained to her that he had seen a wolf in the night and advised her to keep a close eye on her animals. Danli then warned the children at supper to remain vigilant. Mia stopped her nighttime sojourns, yet she missed the graceful, powerful sleekness and muscle of her body after it changed.

∞∞∞

Years passed by. Mia stayed with Danli, becoming an experienced shepherdess, as good and intuitive with the animals as any who'd been born and raised in Dakoris. Mia thought less and less of her childhood on the island with the family that she would never see again, but she remembered the desire to see the world and its various climes. Someday, Mia longed to go on a journey to observe the jungles of Parem and the deserts and plains. But she didn't feel ready, not yet. After so much upheaval, she stayed in her pleasant, stable life.

Danli's son, Nel, had never moved out or married, and continued to perform daily labors on the property. Cady was still living in the home too, but she and Thom began to talk about getting married in the next few years. Much of Cady's energy these days went toward her love interest and planning their wedding. She and Mia were still friendly, but did not enjoy the deep bond they had at a younger age, before the day when Mia accidentally changed shape in front of her and Thom.

One summer day, Mia sat at the spinning wheel near the window, making a thin string of yarn. She was now seventeen years old, with long slender arms and a swan neck, and her dyed red hair was tied into two long pigtails that hung down over her bosom. Sixteen-year-old Cady, tall and elegant with waist-length marigold-colored hair, stirred beans in the kitchen.

Danli burst through the front door, wide-eyed and panting. "Mia," she insisted, "you have to hide. Come here."

"Hide?"

"Yes, right now. Cady, you just act like you know nothing. Say as little as possible and play along with me. Mia, go in here and be as quiet as a mouse." Danli pulled aside a rug, opened a trapdoor beneath it that led to a storage cellar, and shoved Mia toward it.

"What's going on?" Mia asked. "Why must I hide?"

"No time to explain. I'll let you out as soon as I can. Go!"

Nervous, Mia obediently crawled down into the dusty darkness, where jars of preserved fruits and vegetables and barrels of ale lined the floors and wooden shelves. Danli slammed the trapdoor shut and pulled the thick rug back over it to conceal it. Shortly afterward, there was a loud knock on the door. Josi and her half-wolf daughter both barked. Mia listened to Danli's heavy footsteps crossing overhead as she went to open the door. She kept her body as still as she could, nervous about knocking over a jar.

"Hello, miss," said a muffled voice as Mia listened intently in the darkness. Another set of footsteps made their way in. "Are you Danli Merdas?"

"Yes, sir."

"I am here to ask you some important questions." The man's deep, resonant voice had a thick lilting accent that sounded all too familiar. The way Mia's own family had talked.

"What is this about?"

"By any chance, do you have a young woman who lives or stays on your property and has traits of the Kai'Zi race? Silver hair, for instance?"

"No, I do not."

"How many people live here?"

"Myself, my son Nel who still lives here and hasn't married, and my niece Cady who's in the kitchen. Her soon-to-be husband will move in at some point, or she'll be moving out—we haven't decided yet."

"Can you please bring Cady over here?"

Mia heard the lighter tread of Cady's hesitant footsteps, drawing closer.

"Turn around, young lady. Let me see your hair. Turn just once more, that way. Very good. Doesn't look Kai'Zi to me. You're certain that this is the only female besides yourself who resides here?"

"Yes, sir."

"And you are certain that there is not a silver-haired girl around here—or perhaps one who conceals her silver hair with red hair dye?"

"I do entertain guests sometimes, and several are redheads. You're in Dakoris; red hair, whether dyed or not, is everywhere. My younger sister also comes to visit, and she dyes her hair red as well. I can assure you she's every bit as much of a Dakor as I am."

"Miss Merdas, thank you for your time. We'll be on our way." The heavy footsteps trotted out of the house, and hoofbeats faded away.

Several minutes passed before Danli finally pulled the rug off the trapdoor and let Mia out of the stuffy little storage space.

"What was that about?" Mia wanted to know, wide-eyed and visibly shaken. Cady, silent, huddled close to her.

"Aunt Danli," Cady whispered, "who was that man? I saw him riding down the road perhaps a year ago."

"He's been lingering around here for at least a year? This isn't good. Cady, Mia, that man was from Loriar, and he looks to be in the military. And I believe he's here for Mia."

"But why?" Mia begged.

"If I explain, it would cause upset and confusion. It is best to know as little as possible. Mia, I am very sorry, but I can no longer keep you here."

"But I want to stay here!" Tears gathered at the corners of Mia's eyes. "Why must I leave?"

"For your own safety, in case they come back looking for you, or go asking questions amongst the neighbors. If they haven't already. It may look even more suspicious that you weren't in sight. Beginning tomorrow, we're going to head north, and I'm going to leave you with my friends Mendy and Tak."

"But I don't understand."

"There are people looking for you, Mia. And if they find you, nothing good will come of it. Please just trust my judgment here. Say your goodbyes to Cady, Thom, and Nel, and be ready to leave in the morning."

"They think I'm Kai'Zi, don't they? And I'm not of that race, am I?"

"Oh, of course you're not."

"Then why don't we tell them they've got the wrong idea?"

"Sometimes, when people get a particular idea caught in their head, they don't listen to reason."

Mia went around hugging Danli, Cady, Thom, and even Nel, who looked away and stiffened at her touch. After bedtime, Mia lay sobbing in her bed as Cady sat at the edge of the mattress, patting her shoulder.

"Cady, do you have any idea what's going on, or why exactly I have to leave?" Mia sniffled.

"I'm afraid I don't know any more than you do," Cady replied. "Aunt Danli won't talk about it."

"It's just... strange."

"If there is some man following us and looking for you, then I think it's for the best that Aunt Danli is doing this, to be honest. That man didn't look like he had good intentions. He even put his hands on me, lifting my hair, feeling my skin."

"The man must have been very unsettling. But it hurts that I'm suddenly being cast away like this." Even after four years off the island, Mia was apprehensive about the world that lay beyond this scenic patch of land in the mountains. She'd daydreamed about seeing it, but was not quite ready, and felt sick at the thought of being forced out of her safe zone.

"Cady, do you think we'll see each other again after tomorrow?" Mia asked, not sure if she even wanted to know the answer.

"Oh, of course," Cady said in a soothing yet unsure tone. "I'm sure we'll be able to work out a visit, even if I have to sneak up to Tak and Mendy's."

∞∞∞

At sunrise the next morning, Danli woke Mia, fed her a quick breakfast of porridge, and led her out to the stables. Packs containing Mia's few personal belongings and some stores of food were attached to the two horses they would ride. They set out northward onto a road that did not get heavy traffic, faint in the rock and dry grass. Though Tak and Mendy had visited Danli over the years, Mia had never been up north to stay with them before.

It was noon when Mia and Danli stopped to rest, feed and water the horses, and eat. There was no town in sight. They sat underneath a spindly tree beside a creek and snacked on bits of cheese. And then they set on their way, resting on their saddles in an awkward silence.

The journey took four days as the rugged mountainous landscape gradually flattened out and turned to rocky wind-beaten plains and meadows. During the nights, Danli found villages, some tiny and almost forgotten, some larger. Even the more obscure towns, filled with abandoned, half-collapsed skeletons of wood houses, had inns, where the two spent their nights. Whenever Danli checked the two of them into an inn and pushed a fistful of coins over the wooden counters, she encouraged Mia to keep her head down, say nothing, and make eye contact with no one. They ate rushed meals and retired to the bedroom quarters as soon as they could.

On the final day of the journey, as Mia and Danli rode at a walking speed, Mia's skin began to prickle unpleasantly. They trotted their way across a vast plain rife with wildflowers. Storm clouds edged the sky, above mountains and peasants' farms not far off. Mia turned around to look back over her shoulder and noticed a dark figure on a horse, far off, barely perceptible.

"Danli," Mia warned. "I think someone's following us."

Danli glanced behind her. "I can't be sure if they are following us or just going the same way as us," she muttered. "I think it's the latter, but we can't be so sure. Let's run."

They both urged their horses to gallop. The wind blasted the hood of Mia's cloak off her head and whipped at her long braids, freeing strands of hair. She hung on tight to the reins. This being her first time atop a running horse, Mia was afraid of being thrown off. She gritted her teeth as her face grew paler. The thundering hooves kicked up small clouds of dirt.

When Danli finally allowed the horses to relax at a walking pace again, Mia glanced behind her. She thought she could still see that mysterious rider far off, now nothing more than a dark speck. Or perhaps it was just one of the black rocks and boulders that were tossed around on the plains from violent volcanic eruptions many eons ago.

Just as the sun was going down, Danli and Mia came upon a wooden house with large windows, rising up on the flat plain. Danli knocked on the door, and it opened. Danli's friend Mendy, short and strawberry-blonde just as Mia remembered, stood at the other side in a worn gray dress.

"Hello, Mendy," said Danli. "How are you and Tak and your boys doing?"

"Fine, I suppose. It's been a while since I've received a letter from you, Danli. What's with the sudden visit? And you brought her along?" She glanced at Mia with her greenish-blue eyes.

"I didn't have time to write. I do apologize, but this situation is urgent."

Mendy nodded, a knowing and serious expression crossing her face. "Why don't the two of you come inside?"

After they put their horses in the stables and went in, Mia was left sitting in front of the large cobblestone hearth while Danli, Mendy, and Mendy's tall, rugged-looking husband, Tak, went to the main bedroom, closed the door behind them, and spoke in whispered tones. Tak and Mendy's four sons, who ranged in age from eight to seventeen, all still lived at home. The freckled boys shyly nodded and said hi to Mia as they passed by, doing their household chores.

Later, Danli's tall thin form crouched next to Mia's in front of the roaring fire. "You're going to be well taken care of, I promise."

"How long will I be staying here?" Mia asked, distinctly uncomfortable in this strange house.

"As long as you need. They will do everything they can to keep you safe." Danli's eyes looked moist. "Mia, it's been a pleasure living with you. You are a very smart and kind young lady and you've made yourself very useful. Thank you for your years of helping me. I will miss you. Now we'd better eat."

Tak and Mendy's dinner table was a noisy place. Their youngest boys bickered with each other and whined about the blobby goat liver on their plates until the older sons shouted at them to shut up and eat. And then the parents snapped at all of them to quit quarreling. "Can't we have one damned supper in peace?" Tak said through his teeth.

Because Tak and Mendy had no space for Mia in their bedrooms, she and Danli slept out in the main living area in woolen bedding. When the sun came up, Danli woke Mia and said goodbye to her, hugging her almost painfully hard. As Danli went out the front door, tears wet her cheeks, glittering in the dawn light. Mia's heart sank as Danli rode away into the brightening morning.

∞ ∞ ∞

Staying with Tak and Mendy was nowhere near as peaceful or pleasant as the life Mia had enjoyed at Danli's farm. She found the entire family noisy, stressful, bothersome, and a bit unfriendly despite Danli's insistence that these were good and trusted friends. Their cooking was much worse than Danli's and she hated the taste of their gristly meat and gamey liver and over-boiled vegetables. Yucky food aside, the couple's screaming arguments jangled Mia's nerves. Nearly every night, like clockwork, Tak and Mendy began to quarrel with each other over money or chores. Sometimes the fights began at dinner; sometimes they boiled over after bedtime. It was after they closed their bedroom door that the shouting got louder and more distressing, even though Mia could no longer clearly hear their muffled yet venomous words.

"I hope I'm not the cause of all this arguing and tension," Mia sighed one night while sitting before the hearth, as the couple's eight-year-old son, Declan, curled next to her, playing with a ball attached by a string to a wooden cup. Repeatedly, he swung the ball, trying unsuccessfully to land it in the cup. From down the hall, the nightly shouting match roared louder and louder.

"I don't think it's got anything to do with you," Declan assured her. "All they ever do is fight. I'm sick of it. I used to think it was my fault too. But my brothers said it started before I was born."

Not long into Mia's stay, Tak left for the day, riding his horse into the nearest town to run errands. Mendy, standing over the woodstove and ladling a stew simmering with nearly-spoiled ingredients, asked Mia to go outside and feed the family's goats. As Mia tossed hay into their troughs, a presence snuck up behind her. A pair of arms wrapped around her as her nose filled with the sweaty body odor of the oldest son, Tak Junior.

"You're the prettiest girl I've ever seen," he cooed into her ear as his hands reached up and cupped her breasts, squeezing them through her dress. "You're just darling."

Numb and frozen, Mia was back on the island, twelve years old again, smelling the salty breeze and the moist trees as her brother Deto forced his slimy kiss on her. Her muscles grew heavy, as if they turned to stone.

Tak Junior's rough, calloused hands worked their way into the neckline of Mia's dress. Mia's stomach turned as she looked down in fear and shame. Suddenly, he pulled his hands away and backed off when his mother yelled out the window. "Stew's ready!"

That evening, just before dinner, Tak returned with a haul of food and supplies. After the meal, the boys went outside to play and do chores. Mia passed the kitchen as Tak and Mendy cleaned up after dinner and caught a snippet of their conversation. For once, they weren't screaming, instead speaking in a carefully controlled almost-whisper. Mia flattened herself against the wall and quietly listened, knowing the topic was her.

"Did you check the orphanage?" Mendy asked.

"Yes, I did. They said they're full and she's too old besides."

"Too old? I had a feeling that would happen."

"Yup, because she's at an age when girls get married. As if we can just find her a husband on the spot."

"That's too bad. And we don't want the girl marrying our son, do we?"

"Definitely not!"

"We need to think of something else."

"I wonder why you agreed to take her in the first place."

"Danli looked frightened. Desperate."

"You and your goddamned guilt got us in this mess," Tak growled. "But I paid a visit to a certain fellow and got some pretty convincing papers."

"Are you still thinking of that crazy plan?"

"I think it could work. Honest."

"It's risky."

"But think of how it'll help all of us."

As they turned and walked toward the entrance to the kitchen, Mia scurried out of the hall. That night, she tossed and turned on her pallet in the main room, trying uneasily to get to sleep. She did not enjoy overhearing that Tak had tried to talk an orphanage into accepting her. Danli had assured Mia that these people would take care of her for as long as needed. Was there a miscommunication somewhere along the way? Or did no one actually care about Mia?

The nightly fight between Tak and Mendy was especially bad that evening, the shouting so loud that Mia could make out a few of the words Tak yelled in his deep voice: "go there," and "the girl." Out of Mendy's mostly unintelligible screaming, Mia heard her name and "danger." Tak argued back, some sentence containing the word "money." Mia burrowed deeper into her bedding, overcome with an awkward shame.

The second-oldest son banged on their bedroom door, pleading in his cracking adolescent voice: "Ma! Pa! We're trying to sleep!"

"Go back to your room!" his father's voice boomed. "This is a private discussion!"

After that, thankfully, the argument died down and the house was at peace. Still, Mia rolled restlessly on her pallet.

The next day, Mia was asked to feed the goats again, and then feed horses in the stable. She kept her wits about her, but then got caught by surprise. As she turned to leave the stable, Tak Junior stood in the doorway, sneering and blocking her path.

"Let me through," Mia said firmly.

"You're mine now." Tak Junior crept toward her and wrapped her in a suffocating bear hug. She struggled, jabbing at him with her elbows.

"Calm down," he snarled. "If you stop squirming, it'll be much easier for you."

"I don't want you," Mia shouted, finally breaking free from his arms and darting off frantically toward the doorway.

Tak Junior reached out quicker than Mia could move and gripped her upper arm, pinching it in his fingers. She nearly fell as her feet skidded on the hay. Her mind only on her disgust and rage, she balled her free hand and spun around. Her fist met Tak Junior's face. The soft part of his nose crunched against her knuckles as his hand fell away from her arm. Tak Junior bent down, screeching and groaning, as she fled to the house.

Mia came inside, panting, as Mendy cooked another batch of porridge. A few minutes later, Tak Junior followed, blood running from his nose and dripping onto the front of his tunic. Mendy abandoned her pot and held a cloth to his face to stem the bleeding. "What's happened to you, my son?"

Nearby, Mia trembled as she waited for him to rat her out, the way her brother did. Waited to find what sort of trouble she'd get into.

"Oh... uh... I tripped and fell," Tak Junior mumbled, balling up the bloodstained cloth and slipping away to his bedroom.

∞ ∞ ∞

"You're coming on a journey with us," Tak informed Mia over breakfast two mornings later, after the boys had left the table to do chores.

"A journey? Where?"

"To Loriar in the north. It will take quite a while to get to the capital, but we have an inheritance waiting for us there. We have not claimed it yet. We've been stuck here, raising our children, rearing the animals, and it's such a long way to travel. But the time has come to finally make that trip. And we would appreciate your help in coming along, since you've got nothing better to do. We will be very comfortable after we claim the money."

"Loriar... isn't that quite a long way?" Mia reflected on Danli's maps of the western world.

"Yes. But we have good horses, a lot of food and supplies,

and a good map."

"Will your boys be coming?"

"No, it would be too overwhelming. Our oldest sons will be running the house, taking care of the younger two and the animals until we're back. Tak Junior has no prospects of marrying or moving out anytime soon. My sister, who lives down the road, will help them out. We'll be leaving this morning. You need to pack your things."

"Danli told me that this man who came looking for me was from Loriar. I'm not sure why, but she was scared to keep me after that. Will there be other people looking for me? Will it be dangerous for me in Loriar?"

Tak and Mendy exchanged a look that Mia couldn't quite decipher, and then Tak spoke. "Oh, no, it won't be dangerous. There are a few... lunatics... looking for you, but we shall protect you."

"You won't want to stand out, though," Mendy added. "Before we get to Loriar, we'll want to dye your hair black. The people will look down upon you if you have red hair."

"Yet everyone here in Dakoris wants red hair?" Mia was puzzled. "Does every single country have its own hair color that everyone wants? Is there a country where everyone dyes their hair green? Or purple?"

"Haha, no. Up in Loriar, very few people are born with red hair, so they think it is an oddity. We'd best hurry up and finish our food."

Mia never knew what to expect of her life anymore—lately it seemed to be in constant transition, and none of this instability was her idea. It had all started when that military man came to Danli's house, making her skittish about keeping Mia there any longer. Mia's stomach tightened in unease and she had difficulty stuffing down the rest of her breakfast of meat and potatoes. Mia had no other place to go, since her entire immediate family was dead, she did not know of any living relatives or where they might be, she owned no property, and she had no husband on the horizon. The unpleasant alternative to not going on this suddenly announced trip up to Loriar was staying behind in the house with Tak Junior. While his younger brothers were not bad to spend time with, she certainly did not want to find herself alone with the first-born son again.

Once breakfast was finished, Tak and Mendy gathered together four horses, three for riding and one pack horse they had just purchased from a neighbor. They placed dried food, water canteens, fire-building materials, and tents in the packs for occasions when night was falling and an inn might not be nearby. Tak also packed a cudgel, knife, and crossbow with bolts. Mia was a bit nervous to ask why, and hoped the weapons were just to kill animals for food along the way.

Tak and Mendy hugged all four of their sons goodbye.

"Take good care of your brothers and the animals!" Mendy reminded Tak Junior. "And if you need help and company, call on your auntie. We will be gone quite a while, but we will return as soon as we can, and you won't believe how much better life is going to be."

"You won't be back soon enough," Tak Junior growled, clearly unhappy about all the housework and childcare responsibilities suddenly heaped on his shoulders.

As Mia followed Tak and Mendy northward on the faint horse trail that Danli had used to bring Mia to their house, the silence was awkward. All of the steadiness and comfort in Mia's life had been blown to pieces, but at the same time, she realized that this was her opportunity to finally get around to doing something she'd dreamed of on the island of her girlhood: seeing the world.

On the first night of their journey, they found a small village populated by peasants, where the sheep and goats outnumbered the human beings. They checked into the small, ramshackle two-room local inn. Tak spent a few coins and after eating a mediocre dinner, they slept in bunk beds filled with itchy, poking straw. After the candles were blown out, Tak began to snore. Mendy jabbed him awake.

"Quit that snoring," she snarled, waking Mia in the bunk

above.

"I wasn't snoring," Tak protested in a voice heavy and still half-asleep.

"Yes, you were. You sounded like a pig in a trough."

"How many times do I have to tell you? I don't snore!"

"Yes you do, and it's terrible! Now, if only you could stop denying it!"

This is going to be a long trip, Mia thought to herself wearily, rolling over onto her side.

"Shut up!" the stranger in the bunk bed on the opposite wall snapped. "Some of us are trying to sleep!"

"Sorry," Mendy apologized. "It's just that with my husband's loud snoring, I'm the one who gets not a wink of sleep."

"And neither will I with a wife who won't shut up," Tak sighed. "Please, for the love of the sheep-goddess."

Mia dreamt of the island that night—of being back with her family, all still alive. Including Lata, the firstborn, now well into adulthood. In the alternate reality of this dream, Lata had never broken her leg and never gotten the fever that claimed her life when Mia was a young child. Lata smiled the widest, her angelic round cheeks speckled with a few freckles, her hair light brown and curly. The whole family welcomed Mia back with open arms, and Mia's brother Deto told her he was sorry for being disgusting to her and promised not to let it happen again. In the morning, after waking up in the scratchy, uncomfortable bed, Mia remembered that they were all dead and had been for years. Here she was again in the real world, at the mercy of other people's wanderlust and snap decisions.

The next day was spent riding, headed straight toward the ring around the earth. The arch looked a bit bigger now than it did at Danli's house—or was that Mia's imagination? The following night, they stayed at another inn, nestled against the edge of a dense forest. This time, thankfully, Mia was allowed her own room, and a mud-and-straw wall muffled the argument about Tak's snoring.

The next day, they rode into the forest, a mossy haven of velvet green. Unlike the pine and fir forests around Danli's home, this one was filled with deciduous trees—beech, poplar, oak, maple, and apple, shrouded in delicate mists. Rabbits hopped out of sight into the moist grass and lush berry bushes and tree roots, and a deer loped across their path up ahead.

"Isn't this place just charming?" Mendy exclaimed, riding between Tak and Mia and turning her head to admire the canopy of trees. "Just so lush and green. Imagine the red and yellow leaves in the fall! Had we left a little later, we could have seen those colors."

"It really is very pretty," Mia agreed. She still missed the evergreen forests and craggy snow-capped peaks, however.

"It isn't so charming when so much grass grows and so few folks travel this way that you can barely see the trail," Tak growled. "I'm not sure we're on the right path. And it'll go on for days. I hate this forest already."

"You don't have to be so grumpy and gloomy!" Mendy admonished. "Just..."

"Not now!" Tak yelled. "Just give me some peace and quiet so I'll know where we're going!"

"Excuse me for breathing!" Mendy sighed.

Grunting, Tak reached underneath his cloak and removed his map, checking the sky for the sun and the ring, and also glancing at the trees for the side the moss grew on. "All right. We are on the correct trail."

Mia's mind wandered as the easy pace of the horses lulled her. At about midday, Tak veered off the trail and located a wide babbling brook. Fresh water, rushing from the melted snow further south in the mountains, ran icy and clear over smoothed round stones of many colors. The horses happily slurped up the cold water as the humans gathered it in bowls and canteens and did the same. After the horses grazed and Tak, Mendy, and Mia ate a lunch of bread and cheese, they were on their way. As evening set in, the shady environment under the trees grew dim, tinged with a magical-looking lavender mist. Crickets loudly chirped.

"Where are we going to stay tonight?" Mia asked, seeing nothing but trees in all directions.

"We're sleeping here in the woods," Tak told her. "I'm looking for a nice little meadow. We'll want to camp away from the trail."

It didn't take long for Tak to select a beautiful clearing speckled with white and purple wildflowers. He hitched the four horses to trees and then sent Mia out to gather the driest fallen branches she could find for firewood, warning her to not stray too far because it was easy to get lost. Yet as Mia wandered in search of wood, she couldn't help but explore her surroundings a bit and enjoy the peace of nature. Not too far off, the crystal-clear stream gurgled. A breeze rushed through the quaking trees.

After Tak and Mendy built the fire, they hung an iron pot over it and boiled a dinner of potato stew, which they ate from their wooden bowls. Nearby, the horses snorted and grazed. As she often did, Mia found the silence unsettling, and was unsure how to break the unspoken tension between the unhappily married couple.

"When were we going to set up our tents?" Mia finally asked.

"Tonight I won't bother," Tak explained. "The weather is pleasant with no clouds, so we'll just bring out the blankets. On that island, you probably just slept on the sand, right?"

"Not quite. We built these little wooden shelters to sleep in. At first, we had shelters built from parts of a ship... I believe it was the ship my family was on that wrecked. Those shelters blew down in a hurricane."

"What is a hurricane?" Mendy asked.

"A terrifying sort of storm. Very bad, howling winds, strong enough to blow down trees. Pounding rains. I've lived through a few of them."

"That does sound horrible. I thank the sheep-goddess for the decent weather we have here in Dakoris, even if it gets bitter cold."

After setting up their blankets on the ground and stuffing rolled-up blankets underneath their heads for pillows, they bedded down around the warmth of the fire coals.

"I'd like to remind you ladies that that there's a few bears in these woods," Tak informed them. "It's the reason I cleaned the dishes right away and left them to dry far from the camp. If you hear anything funny, let me know."

"Thank you for making me think about bears right before it's time to go to sleep," sighed Mendy.

Mia had never seen a bear, but she'd heard about them from Cady: fearsome big animals with long fangs and claws. Long after Tak started to softly snore, Mia could scarcely fall asleep with the notion of bears now festering in her head. Each time a twig snapped, she stiffened. A chill ran over her body at the plaintive sound of a far-off wolf howl, even though, unbeknownst to Tak and Mendy, she'd generated such howls herself. Mia periodically glanced around. The faint moonlight gave her enough illumination to see far off into the trees. Every time she turned her head, she half-expected shining eyes and fanged jaws.

Even though no bear came to eat them or their horses in the night, Mia was tired the next day. Mendy, who'd been kept awake by similar anxiety, was also sleepy. After they washed their bodies with soap in the ice-cold brook, packed their things, and continued on into the woods, Mia found her eyes slamming shut as they rode. She was afraid of falling asleep and sliding sideways off the horse. Mia found that if she closed her eyes briefly, she could take catnaps while still sitting upright in the saddle. These woods seemed to go on and on, but now they were broken up by occasional sunny clearings with vine-draped homesteads and small herds of sheep grazing in the damp grass.

That evening, after Tak and Mendy found another secluded little hollow to set up camp, their bickering began again. It came as a relief to Mia when Tak sent her out to gather firewood. The shouts got louder as Mia nearly ran off into the trees, trying to escape. Her nerves calmed and her mood lifted with the soothing, balmy summer breeze. Pillars of sun pierced through the branches, slanting sideways in the evening and speckling the plush grassy forest floor.

When Mia got back to the camp, arms loaded with branches, she found Mendy throwing a temper tantrum, tossing potatoes from a burlap bag down to the ground and stomping on them. "Are you happy now?" she screamed at Tak. "You'll never have to eat my terrible cooking again! Happy now? Huh? Huh?"

"You're wasting our food, you ignorant wench!"

"Stop it!" Mia cried in a shrill voice. The couple both turned to stare at her.

"I was... wondering where you'd gone," Tak said awkwardly.

"Why do you shout at each other so much?" Mia said. "I thought we needed those potatoes."

"Don't tell me what to do!" Mendy screeched. However, after pausing, she bent down to pick up the round vegetables she hadn't smashed and then walked in her waddling gait to a nearby creek to wash them. Meanwhile, Tak sat down on a large, lopsided, lichen-mottled rock and patted its side, motioning for Mia to come have a seat. Nervously, she did.

"Mendy's just in a mood," he said in a voice weary from his latest marital squabble. "Don't mind her. We're getting closer to Dakor City, which is on the banks of the Great Parem River. We'll get ourselves and the horses some space on a large boat and travel along the river into Parem. The river flows northeast, so it'll be a faster way to get to where we're going. On the riverboat, I want all of us to keep a low profile, you included. And in case anybody asks your name, tell them that you're called Nori Tethlo."

"But why?"

"To be careful, in case those strange men who followed you and Danli are on our trail. If we are crossing a border between countries and you get asked for your papers, show them this." He reached into one of his bags, dug around, and drew out folded parchment. Mia opened and examined it. In quill ink, it was written that she was Nori Tethlo, aged seventeen, born in Korus, Dakoris. An official-looking wax stamp and illegible signature graced the bottom of the document.

That night underneath her blanket, the thought of ferocious bears still made Mia's skin tingle, though with her sleep deprivation the night before, she drifted off more quickly. Mia awoke with a start in the dead of night, sensing something wrong in the air. She couldn't tell what made her prickle all over with unease. Mia sat up, gathering her blanket around herself, and surveyed her surroundings. Off in the distance was an irregularity between two trees, something that didn't look quite like it belonged. Something moved, something black and long-haired—the swish of a horse's tail. And that horse wasn't one of the four that traveled with her party.

Mia slid all the way out of her bedding and crept barefoot across the soft soil and cool grass. Hiding in the trees, she walked quietly toward the horse and discovered a camp with just a few sacks on the ground, no signs of a campfire. Underneath a blanket, an unfamiliar-looking man slept soundly, his face dark with stubble. Armor hung off a tree nearby. Poking out from the stranger's bedding was the glinting hilt of a sword. It occurred to Mia that this man had probably chosen not to start a fire because he wished to stay hidden.

His horse, still awake, turned its head and spotted Mia standing in the darkness with its gleaming eye. Startled, it tossed its head and whinnied loudly. Mia ran as fast as she could back to her own campsite. She shook both Tak and Mendy awake, whispering. "There is a man with a sword sleeping nearby. I'm frightened that I might have woken him."

"Let's stay quiet," Tak muttered, frantically reaching into a bag he kept near his blanket and fumbling around. After some groping, he pulled out his crossbow. Mendy grabbed a lamp, lighting it with a coal from the fire.

Not far off, a twig cracked.

"What's out there?" Mendy whispered in an anxious squeak. "I can't see!"

"I don't know!" Tak gripped his crossbow hard.

In the field of Mia's superior night vision, the stranger was coming straight at them, eyes hard and determined. He had his long sword drawn, gripped in his hand. A length of rope dangled from his belt.

"He's coming with his sword!" Mia whispered, pointing with a shaking finger.

Tak aimed the crossbow. "Where is he?"

"Right there!"

The man stepped out from behind a tree, now close enough that Tak and Mendy caught the glint of his sword in the dim light of Mendy's lamp. Tak fired the crossbow. With a gasp and a groan, the stranger collapsed backwards.

Tak crept over toward the fallen man, struggling and moaning in pain as the bolt protruded from his stomach and blood trickled down his side. Mia followed him as Mendy stayed behind, keeping her blanket wrapped around her body. Pulling his knife from its sheath, Tak slit the man's throat and watched him gag as he bled out into the dirt.

"Sorry you had to see that," Tak apologized as they rushed back to the camp, "but that fellow was up to no good. Had to make sure he was dead."

Tak returned with the lantern and waved it over the dead man, peeking around at his clothing. He felt and patted around at the belt, finding no bags attached.

"Mia," Tak asked, "can you show me where he slept?"

Tak kept his crossbow out as Mia led him to the spot where the brown horse was still tied to a tree, snorting. Tak bent down and rifled through a small knapsack lying on the ground next to the pallet. He drew out a piece of parchment and held the lantern up to it.

"He was Karot Throll, from the Loriar military. I knew he was Loriar from the style of his vest."

"What was he doing here? Could he have had anything to do with that Loriar man who visited Danli and got her so spooked?"

"I've got no clue. Ah, well, it looks like he was here alone, but we'd best keep an eye out for other nutcases like him."

Tak picked up a sack of the dead man's food and supplies, figuring he, Mia, and Mendy could use them on their journey. They crept back to camp, carefully stepping around the body and the circle of blood-soaked soil surrounding it.

It was hard for all of them to sleep for the rest of that night. The scent of blood lingered in Mia's nose as her ears listened carefully for any suspicious sounds. They slept late in the morning, warmed by the sun's rays. After waking, they buried the dead Loriar soldier in the earth and left for another day of travel through the idyllic woods, taking the man's horse with them.

When at last they emerged from a wooded patch on the rolling hills that surrounded Dakor City, Mia was amazed. The settlement was nearly as large as the port city of Korus, with the same style of cobblestone buildings and roads, and the Great Parem River split the city in half. Mia had loved her book about the children rafting on the river ever since her oldest sister Lata taught her to read, but it was wider than she'd ever imagined, a huge channel of water that shone white in the sun. Boats docked at both sides of Dakor City, and sailed down the river off into the unknown.

"This is where I grew up," Mendy said with a little sigh. "I haven't been here in years and years."

After Mia, Tak, and Mendy rode into the well-organized streets of the southern half of the city, they got busy running errands. They sold the horse that they had taken from the dead soldier, adding quite a bit to their cash. They reserved space at an inn for that night and a spot on a riverboat that would depart the following morning. After they settled in at the large, well-kept inn, Mendy went shopping for some personal items, including red hair dye to touch up Mia's hair and black dye for her to use later on, before entering Loriar.

Before supper, Mia went to a private room to bathe in a tub of warm, soapy water fragrant with herbs and to refresh the roots of her hair with the new red dye. She resented the hassle of having to color her hair, but she liked the fact that it took unwelcome attention off her.

Yet even after years of being a redhead, that soldier had followed Mia into the nearby woods and was quite possibly the same one who scared Danli into giving her up. Did he think she was a member of an enemy race and want to capture her? Hopefully with him gone, the stalking would end and the rest of this trip would be a peaceful one. And after getting back home to Dakoris, maybe Mia could talk Danli into allowing her to move back in.

As the guests gathered at a long wooden table to dine on an array of meat, fruit, and ale, Mia and Mendy noticed Tak's absence. He never joined them for supper.

After they finished eating and went to their room, Mendy clasped her hands and sat on the soft quilted down-stuffed bed. "Mia, I'm getting worried. You're the one who can see well in the dark, and the sun is going down soon. Can you find where Tak is?"

"How far should I go?"

"Don't stray too far or get lost. I'll follow."

As Mia went looking for her traveling companion, Mendy a few steps behind, the skirt of her simple dress swished around her legs and her thick damp braid swung behind her. The humidity made Mia feel a bit sticky under the dress. This part of Dakoris was decidedly hotter and wetter than the part she was accustomed to living in. She'd barely noticed the moisture of the island after growing up there, but now she was used to a drier mountain climate.

"Oh, dear," Mendy whispered. "It looks like we chose an inn right on the edge of a bad part of town. I haven't been here in so many years, I'd forgotten this was a rough district."

The streets crawled with people and it was hard to spot Tak if he was around. As she went down some streets, the action inside the buildings grew too loud. Mia peeked through a pair of open wooden double doors to a pub, where crowds of people tossed back cups of ale.

There he was—Tak, loudly laughing with a group of sloppy-looking, dirty-faced men. When Mia leaned into the smelly, crowded pub and called his name, he did not show signs of hearing her voice through the thick wall of noise.

"Mendy!" Mia called, looking over her shoulder. "There he... Mendy?"

Mendy was gone. Somewhere along the busy street, they had gotten separated.

When Tak came out, he was in the middle of a raucous crowd that brusquely pushed Mia aside. She fell backwards, and then brushed the dirt off her dress and pursued Tak into the dimming night. She again lost track of Tak, and his wife was still nowhere to be found. Mia paced up and down the streets, through squares of light from noisy bars and inns.

Mia peeked into one trash-filled alley between two closed shops. Two figures were pressed against a stone wall. Sneaking into the darkness and flattening herself against the wall behind a sack of smelly garbage buzzing with flies, Mia recognized Tak's red-gold hair and craggy facial profile. A giggling woman was sandwiched between Tak and the wall, her hair gathered up in messy coils and her dress pulled up to the waist, exposing her parted legs. Tak backed away from her. The woman let her skirt fall back down as Tak fastened the front of his pants closed. He dropped a few coins into her hand, she nodded to him in thanks, and then they both dashed out of the alley, Tak not noticing Mia crouched in the shadows.

Her stomach turning, Mia ran back toward the inn, screeching to a halt when she finally located Mendy, wandering up and down the street. She led Mendy by the arm back toward where she'd last seen Tak. They bumped into him as he stumbled drunkenly, his clothing disheveled. Mendy's face turned bright red and twisted into a hideous expression of rage. Her fingernails dug into Tak's skinny arm as she dragged him back to the inn with her and Mia. The fight began even before they reached the room the three of them would share that night, and the volume increased after the door closed.

"You never change!" Mendy wailed, throwing her hands all around. "How much of our hard-earned money did you spend on drinks and whores? Give me that coin purse!"

The shouting got even louder as Mendy rifled through the coins and found many of them gone. "We'll scarcely be able to buy food after we get off the boat, you lying, cheating, blundering idiot!" she wailed as Mia escaped from the room, head down. Not sure where else to go, she sat at the table in the main dining area and fidgeted uncomfortably.

Tak came down some time later and sat down next to her, biting his lips, his expression tight with tension. "I cannot believe you followed me and ratted me out," he snarled at Mia.

Mia instinctively flinched. "I... I'm sorry," she mumbled. "But Mendy was worried that you had missed supper. We had to go look for you."

"She won't speak to me now," Tak growled, pumping his fists and staring forward. "You damn near ruined my marriage. Hell, you might've ruined it outright."

Mia's anxiety turned to anger. Her hurt and frustration moved her enough to speak up for once. "With all due respect," she cautiously pointed out, "you are the one who spent the money and sneaked off with that woman, and neither of you seems happy in your marriage to begin with."

"You don't care for a man's privacy at all! I just ought to..." He grabbed Mia by her braid, yanking it painfully, and pulled her off the wooden bench. She felt herself back on the island, with the smell of sea salt breezing by, the rage of her parents in her face.

"Come with me, Mia!" Tak barked. "It's over!"

"Don't... do... it!" came Mendy's voice from the doorway, loud and stern and clear. The few others remaining in the dining room turned to stare.

"But this brat here..."

"Just don't do it! Think, Tak! Just sit and think! Let that girl go right now!"

Mia backed away, patting herself and gasping, as Tak released her long shining red braid from his hand. Mendy took Tak by the arm and led him back to the room.

Mia did not feel safe going back with them. She lingered in the torchlit dining hall, watching a few travelers drink cups of ale, until Mendy returned for her, insisting that she go to bed.

"Tak isn't going to hurt me?" Mia asked Mendy, wide-eyed.

"No, he's not. He just lost his temper. He is over it now. We need to get up early for the boat tomorrow."

∞∞∞

The riverboat was not as big as the ship that had rescued Mia, but big enough to hold several people and cases of their things, and comfortably accommodate their horses in stalls in the lower deck. As it departed from the south bank of Dakor City and gently rode the current of the Great Parem River, Mia clung to the side railing, looking out over the rushing water and the city, fading away as the homes thinned out and turned into vegetation. The thrill of floating down this massive, legendary river took Mia's mind off the tension between Tak and Mendy, who sat on benches nearby, coldly ignoring each other. The couple hadn't spoken a word between them since getting up that morning, and they'd all gathered their things in a deeply uncomfortable silence. The only thing Tak had said at all, other than "wake up," was a reminder to Mia to go by the name Nori while on the boat. They signed her up for the ride under that fake identity.

Mia's eyes misted with tears as the reality sunk in that they were leaving Dakoris, not to return for quite a while. This lovely country was all Mia had known ever since her arrival from the ocean. She didn't feel ready to say goodbye to the land that became her home.

There was a mix of people on the boat. Some had the long thin faces, fair skin, and plain cloaks common among the Dakor people. Other travelers, natives of Parem, had olive complexions, brown eyes, and curly hair ranging from golden to dark brown in color. Most of them wore dresses or robes zigzagged with red and white patterns. They also seemed fond of heavy bronze jewelry.

By the evening of that first day on the water, Mia developed a slight crush on a young Parem man named Doral. He had large, expressive brown eyes and hair pulled back into a bun with a bronze circlet. Doral was the first to say hello to Mia as she watched the vegetation go by on the far-off shore. When they introduced themselves to each other, she almost gave away her real name before remembering that she was supposed to be called Nori. As he struck up conversation, Mia drank up his friendliness and quickly attached to him. For the first time that she could remember in her life, she did not feel nervous in close proximity to a young male.

Dinner that evening was an unfamiliar feast of Parem foods, mostly the meat of rabbits with a sugared dried snake jerky for dessert. After years of a bland, goat-heavy diet, Mia found the food took some getting used to, particularly the strips of reptile meat. Once the feast was finished, Mia wasted no time in going back out onto the deck to look for Doral. Once she found him, they both leaned against the wooden boat railing, watching the twinkling stars as they talked. The great white arch now took up so much space in the sky that it reminded Mia of life on the island.

"Where do you live?" Mia asked.

"Parmos, where the river empties out into the Losor Ocean. That's where I'm headed—I'll be back home in time for the big yearly festival. Where do you come from?"

"I live out in the country in Dakoris."

"I thought that might be the case."

"Has anyone come with you?" Mia asked.

"No. I went alone to stay with a friend in Dakor City. Now I'm returning to my aunt's house."

"You live with her?"

"Yes."

"Where are your parents?"

Doral looked down and sighed. "I don't remember a lot about them. They both died from the plague when I was small. I was very lucky I didn't catch it. We're fortunate that the rabbit catchers in eastern Parem found a cure. But they figured it out too late to save my parents."

"I'm sorry." Mia didn't quite know what to say. Sudden anger rose up within her as she remembered the story behind that plague, that it was spread by an enemy race from the east. The Kai'Zi. This kindly young man had lost his parents for no good reason thanks to them. Mia had no recollection of the plague, growing up isolated on the island. But seeing the aftereffects firsthand and how it left families permanently changed, including her new friend who'd been orphaned, she hated the people who had done this, those Kai'Zi rats who must have had no conscience.

Mia was about to tell Doral that she was an orphan too. But Mendy walked out onto the deck and vigorously motioned for her to come down to their room.

"I've got to go," Mia said apologetically.

"I understand," Doral assured her with a gentle, handsome smile. "I'll see you tomorrow."

"If that boy asks," Mendy advised Mia right before blowing the candle in their room out, "tell him that we're your mother and father."

"But why? It's already tricky enough to use a false name."

"The less folks wonder about us, the better."

"Mendy?"

"Yes?"

"Are we going all the way to Parmos?"

"No; we didn't pay to go that far. This boat is going to go into a branch of the river and dock at Arlemo. We'll get off there and then continue into the jungle."

"We're going straight through the jungle?"

"Yes. We'll need to if we're to go north. Tak will protect us from harm. It shall be fine."

Parem

Mia only knew where she was when Doral's friend Toro pointed it out. They had crossed the border into the nation of Parem. The vegetation changed into thick, dense rainforest draped with moss and ropy vines. Ferns lined the banks of the river, and the cries of unfamiliar birds and beasts and monkeys could be heard far off. Large, beaked insects came searching for the blood of passengers, who began to spend more time inside, especially during the bug-heavy evenings.

Shortly after crossing the border, the boat docked at a small village and picked up more passengers. One of them was a short, voluptuous Parem woman who chatted with Mia by the rail as the boat glided away from the town.

"So," said the young woman, "you're from Dakoris?"

"Yes."

"I've got a question." She giggled. "Is it true what they say about Dakor men?"

"I'm sorry, I don't follow."

"Are the rumors true?" The girl tittered again and winked.

"What rumors?"

"Well... the men from your country, I've heard that they're, um, quite big. Is that so?"

"They tend to be tall, though many of them are on the skinny side."

"I'm not talking about height and weight, silly."

"I apologize. You have me confused."

"Did you ever date men back home?"

"I've never dated a man."

"Never?! You poor thing! I'm talking about what's in their pants. I've heard those Dakor men are endowed like stallions."

"That's enough!" Mia started to blush. Her ears burned.

"Oh, now. I'm sorry to hear you didn't have a gentleman friend back home. You must be missing out!"

Mia's face continued to redden as the young woman left and struck up a conversation with someone else.

That evening, the passengers were served a stew made with the stringy meat of the Parem tree monkey. Tak and Mendy, who sat beside Mia, still were not on speaking terms. Tak happily gobbled his stew while Mendy sneered in disgust, sickened at the thought of monkey flesh. Mia didn't like the gamey taste and ate around the meat, focusing on the chopped vegetables in the broth.

Doral and his friend Toro sat across from them.

"Nori, this may help your stew taste better," the black-haired Toro suggested to Mia, using her false name. He took the lid off a small pot and handed her three dried, twisted little red peppers.

"Do I drop these in?"

"Or you can simply pop them into your mouth." Toro smiled.

"What are these?"

"Something you'll never find in Dakoris, where your food is dreadfully dull."

The peppers smelled spicy and smoky, and Mia's mouth watered heavily. She lifted one gnarled pepper to her lips, bit into it, and began to chew the crispy flesh and seeds just as Doral looked in her direction. "Nori!" he cried as his eyes went wide. "No!"

"Too late," Toro snickered.

The taste turned into burning pain as the seeds scorched Mia's tongue and the insides of her cheeks. Toro laughed as Mia's eyes watered and her face flushed. She spat the pepper out, yet the heat lingered. Desperate to rid herself of the agony, she gulped down the coconut water from her tankard, and then took Mendy's rum-infused water without asking and chugged that too.

"Toro, what is wrong with you?" Doral yelled. "You gave her a death pepper without warning her?!"

"But it's so funny to see how Dakors handle those! Haha, look how red her face is!"

"Nori, drink this!" Doral handed Mia his water. "Swish it around in your mouth."

Mia attempted to rinse it away, but the sting from the hot pepper still lingered for a long time as tears trickled down her face.

"These young rascals are no friends of yours," said Mendy, patting Mia's shoulder. "Don't take food if you don't know what it is. Come on. Let's go to our room."

After Tak and Mendy blew their candles out and went to sleep in a stuffy silence, Mia still felt restless. She laid awake in bed for a while, waiting for the gentle, constant rocking of the boat to soothe her. It did not. Mia slipped out of bed. This late at night, the bloodsucking insects tended to thin out, so she went up to the deck. The air was thick with silver fog, and phosphorescent plants glowed far off on the river banks. Frogs sang.

Mia spotted Toro and Doral on the deck, leaning against the railing, and joined them.

"Hey, Nori, I'm sorry about giving you that pepper earlier," Toro apologized.

"It's okay," said Mia, looking out at the moonlight reflecting off the glistening river.

"I found something very interesting in my father's bag," Toro said, his eyes narrowing suggestively. "Nori, would you like to see it?"

"I suppose so."

Lantern in hand, Toro led Mia and Doral down the flight of creaky, spongy stairs below deck to the room where Toro was staying by himself, adjoining the chamber where his parents slept. Mia and Doral sat on the narrow bed as Toro pulled a stack of parchment from the leather sack he had stolen from his father. Mia's body tingled with warmth as she sat closer to Doral than she ever had before, nearly close enough to touch. As Doral leafed through the pieces of parchment, Mia peered over his shoulder. She began to blush furiously. Naked, curvaceous women were drawn in great detail in charcoal. Some had their legs spread. The young men's grins widened as Mia's face grew hot in her shock.

"Isn't that something?" Toro asked. "The artist didn't leave out a single detail, did he?"

"What was your father doing with these drawings?" Mia asked.

"He's a man. Men like to look at things."

"I think I've had enough," Mia said, wanting to take her eyes off the pictures. But their forbidden nature was a bit exciting, and she had a hard time not giving them one last glance. Toro turned to face her.

"What was that?!" Toro jerked backwards and stared straight at Mia's face.

"What was what?"

"Her eyes! Doral, have you seen this?"

"Seen what?" Doral leaned toward Mia.

"They shine!"

Doral gasped. "They do shine when the light hits them just right!"

"She has the eyes of a hunter!" Toro shrieked, his voice strangely high-pitched. "Get her out of here!"

"I... what?" Mia asked, surprised.

"Get away from us! Shoo! Shoo!" Toro yanked her off the bed, touched her warily like she was on fire, and shoved her out of the room. While she stood stunned, he closed the wooden door behind her and latched it shut. Mia got no response when she banged on the door.

Mia rushed back up to the deck alone, tears of confusion and humiliation trickling down her cheeks. Standing at the rail, not noticing Mia, Tak was speaking with a short woman, the same young lady who'd gossiped with Mia earlier about the rumored endowments of Dakor men. Now it seemed that she wanted to find out firsthand if it was true. The traveler flirted shamelessly with Tak, thrusting her hips about and giggling. He reciprocated with body language just as seductive as hers. For a split second, Mia thought about stopping them, but it would do nothing but make Tak angry. She could get yelled at; she could get her hair grabbed again. So she decided to let the encounter continue, and hope that Mendy wouldn't find out about whatever happened next. It wasn't long before Tak and the young lady slipped to someplace below deck. After giving it a few minutes to make sure they were gone, Mia walked down to the room where Mendy snored alone, unaware of her husband's absence.

Mia quietly cried herself to sleep, still sniffling when Tak finally tiptoed in. Her feelings were still sore the next morning when a few fellow passengers avoided her and whispered in each other's ears when they caught sight of her. Doral passed her on the deck after breakfast, and he averted his eyes as well. Desperate for an explanation if nothing else, she caught him by the arm.

"Why are people acting so funny around me? What are they saying about me?"

"Well, uh... it's Toro," Doral said nervously, darting his eyes from side to side. "He's been going around and saying, well, because of your eyes..."

"What has he been saying?"

"A vampire's eyes shine like yours. He's afraid now."

"A vampire?" Mia gasped, taken aback by the suggestion. "You're saying you people think I'm a bloodsucking creature of the night?!"

"Well, I don't know what to think, and..."

"Get away from him!" Toro shouted, approaching them. "Don't touch him, you animal!"

"I am not a vampire!" Mia insisted loudly. "You two are

being very silly!"

Toro and Doral stared, both tense.

"If I were a vampire, I would melt out here in the sun, now, wouldn't I? But here you see me, standing right in its rays. And I would live on a diet of blood, would I not? But I eat the same things as everyone else. And nobody on this boat has had their blood drank, far as I know. That is... until I go for the neck!" Mia made Toro scream, lunging at him and tilting her head to align with his jugular vein. She laughed at his jumpiness, not even caring anymore what he thought of her.

"Toro, we need to stop this and calm down," Doral urged. "I really don't think she's a vampire. They can't tolerate sunlight, and she's outside every day."

"Well, what is she, then?"

"I think she's just an ordinary girl."

"I still think something's not quite right," Toro insisted. "Come on, Doral. We're getting out of here."

Doral glanced apologetically over his shoulder at her as he and Toro walked away. With a sad sigh, Mia went over to the railing to watch the water go by.

∞∞∞

After how awkward things had gotten, it came as a relief when they docked at the city of Arlemo. Mia still felt drawn to Doral, more so since he had stood up for her to Toro, and she stole a hug from him before they parted, probably to never see each other again. Mendy forcefully dragged Mia away from the boy as the crew unloaded the passengers' horses and donkeys from a smelly compartment below the deck, coaxing the animals out onto a ramp.

Tak and Mendy led Mia and their horses into a network of streets bustling with fruit carts and donkeys. The architecture of Arlemo was unlike anything Mia had ever seen. Black ziggurats, constructed from square stones, rose toward the rainforest treetops, terraced with platforms where grass, rice, and other crops grew. A street festival of some sort was going on. Scantily clad women danced on a few of the lower terraces, swaying their hips in sheer silk skirts and exposing their bejeweled navels. Musicians played lively tunes with carved bone horns, hide drums, and odd stringed instruments.

At the center of the city stood a gleaming black terraced pyramid taller than the others. Glittering, polished bloodred jewels lined the blocky front entrance, which appeared to lead to a staircase that went underground.

"What's that?" Mia asked Mendy.

"That's the house of the town lord."

"What are those pretty red rocks on the door?"

"Some sort of gemstone... what is it again?" Mendy scratched her coiled braids in thought.

"It's the Parem ruby," Tak contributed in the first real words he spoke to his wife in days.

"Oh, that's right!"

"They sell these gems for a lot of money. Women and noblemen in other countries just love to wear 'em."

As the three continued walking, they passed a well-muscled man sitting at the side of the street, holding rough reddish stones up to a spinning metal wheel, operating it with a foot pedal.

"What's he doing?" Mia asked, curious.

"That man is polishing rubies so that they can be nice enough to sell," Tak said.

"They don't come out of the ground shiny and sparkly?"

"No, they look more like ordinary rocks."

"I wouldn't mind polishing rocks for a living," Mia said dreamily. The ruby-polishing machine reminded Mia pleasantly of her days relaxing at Danli's house, spinning wool indoors and happily lost in thought on the days when she was not tasked with herding the sheep.

"I think it would be an awfully dull job," Mendy opined. "You haven't got time to polish rocks. We've got to get to Loriar and we've got a ways to go yet."

They located a stone-walled inn, stabled their three horses, and then did a bit of shopping for food at the fruit carts in the streets. Mendy decided to get a head start on changing Mia's hair color, so that evening, in the spring baths at the back of the inn, she turned it a shiny jet-black and rinsed the gritty dye away with a bucket of cold water. When Mia looked in a mirror in the narrow stone hallway, smooth straight black hair fell, thick and shiny, past her shoulders. She thought that it looked unnatural with her pale skin and ice-blue eyes. She now seemed to have no eyebrows; the silver-white color of the brows disappeared in contrast to the dark hair.

That night, sleep came quickly despite the noise from late-night music and festivities out in the streets. Tak and Mendy didn't even yell at each other. As they ate a breakfast of rice and spiced rabbit jerky before leaving the following morning, Tak and Mendy spoke with fellow travelers.

"You going up north into the jungle?" asked a weathered old merchant with jewels dangling from his ears and a head of wild white hair.

"Yes," Tak confirmed. "Do you know of a less beaten path?"

"Yes, I know of a shortcut where not many travelers go. You go up the main highway—there are plenty of inns along the way—and then you turn at a right fork in the road just after the village of Doren. Most of the jungle is not well-explored and it's easy to get lost, but if you stay on the path, that won't happen. It is a little hard to see in the trees sometimes, but travelers have left little markers… piles of stones you can't miss. If you go that route, please be careful."

"Why?"

"There are some tribes further up north who can be quite territorial. And there are some creatures called ahras. Have you heard of those before?"

"Can't say that I have."

"They live somewhere along that path. The ahras are the reason not many people go that route. You'll know you're in ahra country when you see huge, bright, blue flowers on the ground that have a foul smell like rotting meat. There are monkeys who eat the petals of the flowers, and those petals put them in an altered state. They'll stumble around like they drank too much ale. Ahras feed on those monkeys, which smell just enough like human beings. And, given the opportunity, ahras will eat us, too."

"Oh, my," Mendy gasped.

"They are so fast that you will not even see them. I'm not sure a single person alive knows what an ahra looks like. Those who have seen them don't live to tell about it."

"Oh, dear." Mendy began biting at her nails. "It sounds as if going that way isn't the best idea."

"There is a way to protect yourselves. Ahras hate groups and catch prey alone. Stick by each other's sides at all times. Ride close together. Never let a person go off alone. Even if you must do your private business in the trees, never leave each other's sides until you're certain you're out of ahra country."

"What about the horses?" Tak wanted to know.

"Don't worry about them. I've never heard of ahras eating horse flesh. The ahras live in a narrow strip of country. You'll be out of there before you know it. But please, please be careful."

"We really appreciate you letting us know." Tak thanked the man.

The party of three set out, following a confusing, zigzagged street that led to the north and out of the town of dark stone-block ziggurats. Soon they would be passing under the ring around the earth, which now looked massive, dominating the sky with its ridged white beauty. Mia couldn't wait to see how it looked from directly below. Would she see the deities that lived up there, the God of All and the sheep-goddess, if they existed?

The rainforest was thick at the edges of the main highway, where a few merchants dragged their wooden wheeled carts along the damp ground on foot and oxen pulled larger wagons and carts. When Tak and Mendy and Mia decided to take a lunch break in a clearing, a very chatty merchant decided to join them uninvited, hitching his pair of oxen next to the snorting horses. He sat down on a mossy rock, his brass pieces of jewelry clinking together and his red robe spreading over the stone.

"Where are you all going?" he asked, loudly chewing bread coated with peeled, dried death peppers that made his companion's eyes water just from the smell.

"How can you eat those peppers like it's nothing?" Tak asked, scratching his reddish beard that had grown from lack of shaving.

"Eat these and it makes the weather feel cooler around you," the merchant grinned, his mouth full and his eyes leaking tears. He chased his mouthful with a big gulp from his canteen. "Never stops burning, but it toughens you up. Life's tough anyway. Where are you all going?"

"Up to Loriar. But we, erm, wish to beat the heavy traffic, so we'll be taking a shortcut."

"The path north of Doren?"

"Yes."

"Be careful! You know of the creatures along that stretch, right?"

"Yes, a fellow at the inn warned us."

"I would think carefully before you go that way. I had a buddy take that chance once, and he never came back. All that was left of him was his horse, running out of the jungle in a panic."

"Was he alone?" Tak asked.

"Yeah, he was. I know, that's why the ahras got him, but not everyone realizes that's when they're gonna get you. I've never traveled that path. After my friend disappeared, I'd be too frightened, even if I was in the center of a group of fifty people. Anyone want some of my bread? I've got almost too much." He held up a slice of bread and a drawstring bag of peeled peppers.

"I keep thinking about that pepper I was tricked into eating," Mia spoke up, "and looking back, I actually sort of liked the taste. I might like to try another."

"Are you crazy?" Mendy yelled. "You'll drink all of our water!"

"But it will toughen me up for the road."

"We would also like to have water to drink on the road."

"Oh, come on, let her have some," the merchant encouraged. "No need to concern yourself about water. There's a spring just ahead."

After snacking on hard bread covered with the peeled peppers, Mia found herself enjoying them even more, although she, Tak, and Mendy did have to refill a couple of canteens when they reached the fresh spring.

Days later, they came upon the village of Doren just before sundown. This village was positioned just below the ring. Mia stared in wonder up to the sky and saw nothing but a skinny, glowing strip from the east to the west.

The village was quite a bit smaller than the city of Arlemo, but had similar architecture with ziggurats built of dark blocky stones. Festivities lit up the streets. Small glowing lanterns hung from strings over the damp stone, and heavily jeweled women danced and swayed, their arms waving in the air like snakes. Mia sort of wished to be lost in the dancing and the music, having fun with the other villagers, intoxicated by the glittering and the movement and the joyous laughter. However, Tak and Mendy had just one goal in mind: finding a place to sleep and pushing on, day after day, toward Loriar. Mendy did not allow Tak to go out and party after what he was caught doing in Dakor City.

Unfortunately, the local inn was full. Tak, Mendy, and Mia had arrived too late. Just as they were about to give up and retreat to the surrounding rainforest to camp out, a balding man, wearing a long red dress-like garment, approached them. "You are travelers from Dakoris, aren't you? And the inns are full."

"That's right," Tak sighed.

"My name is Alin. I have an extra room," he offered. "I can let you three stay, as long as you cause no trouble, and I'll charge you less money than the inns would have."

"Sure," Tak readily agreed.

Even though Mia felt a bit of discomfort in the pit of her belly at the thought of staying in this strange man's home, she said nothing. They hitched the horses in the patch of grass and foliage at the back of Alin's small ziggurat, and then they were led to a generously sized stone-lined room down in his basement. A small row of windows stayed open through the night to keep fresh air flowing through and cool things down a bit. Mia, Tak, and Mendy all slept soundly on pallets laid out upon the floor.

The following day started with an argument at breakfast about the day's travel plans.

"Tak," Mendy snarled over her bowl of porridge served by their host, "do you still, in all seriousness, want to go on that trail with the ahras, or whatever those things are called, and risk our lives?"

"We *are* going that way. We've already been told how to keep 'em from eating us. Stick together and it'll be fine."

"But I'm still scared it's dangerous!" Mendy wailed.

Tak's tone grew cold and controlled. "The main highway might not be much safer. I've got a funny feeling that a few oddballs from Loriar might still be trailing us. And that's where they'll look. I'd rather not have to use my crossbow. Or my knife."

Like Mendy, Mia woke up uneasy about the less-beaten trail, but knew that Tak would not listen to her if she brought up her thoughts. Her anxiety worsened as they said goodbye to Alin, left town, and turned onto the narrower road toward the ahra-inhabited territory.

The trail was sometimes hard to see in the thick trees, hanging drapes of moss, and tangles of vines and elevated roots that covered the ground. They kept the horses at a slow walking pace, fearful that one might catch and break a leg in the roots. Even though they did not yet see any of the foul-smelling blue flowers that warned of the presence of ahras, they followed each other very closely just in case.

After about a half day's journey, Tak reached into one

of his sacks for a piece of fruit to eat and made a disturbing discovery. The sack was too light. It no longer contained his coins. Mendy rifled through her bags and found them also devoid of cash.

"The bastard stole our coins!" Tak shouted, his face and the tips of his ears flushing pink. "Alin must have gone through all of our bags while we slept! What a sneak. Let's turn back and get that man for what he's done!"

Immediately, the three of them turned the horses around and headed back to Doren.

By the time they returned to the village, it was the late afternoon, and the sun hung low and orange in the surrounding jungle. When they reached Alin's house, they found it unlocked. In his red-faced rage, Tak swung the heavy stone door open without knocking and paced around the twisted corridors inside, looking for the occupant.

"That bastard is gone!" Tak yelled when he came back out. "And so are half of his things. I did not see a single coin anywhere."

When they talked with neighbors and passers-by, they learned that Alin had left on his mule in the morning, pulling a cart loaded with possessions, telling one of his neighbors that he was moving away. None of them had any idea where. Stranger still, this man had only lived in the home for three months. The neighbors suspected he was a squatter, drifting from place to place, running from something.

"Well, that was a waste of a day," Tak growled, gritting his teeth, as they rode away from town. "That fellow must've been a professional thief, always on the run after he pilfers someone's coins. I've a mind to slit his throat if and when I see him next."

None of them were in the mood to talk about anything else as they rode on, tracing their steps back north. Shortly after getting off the main highway, they decided to pull aside into a small clearing and take a snack break, carefully rationing their food now that they had no money, eating only small pieces of bread and cheese that barely satisfied their hunger.

Still craving food, Mendy spotted red berries hanging from a nearby bush in juicy clusters. Just as she reached for handfuls to pick, Mia stopped her, grabbing her arm. "No!"

"What's wrong with you?" Mendy snapped.

"They're probably poisonous."

"You cannot know just by looking at them."

"Well, I'm not sure if you'd want to find that out the hard way. No animals eat those berries. They're all still on the bush. If they were edible, some of them would be eaten, especially on the bottom."

"Fine. Whatever."

Hoping that the time hadn't come yet to stick together constantly and fear monsters, they took turns slipping into the cover of the thick trees to dig small holes and relieve themselves. When Mia finished, she lowered her dress, kicked dirt over her toileting hole, and then started to daydream as she stared off into the swaying boughs and drapes of moss and long ropy vines. The forest was damp and humid, making her hair strands stick to her dewy cheeks, but it was beautiful and almost enclosed by the leaves above the moss-covered cathedral roots. She wondered what lay beyond, far off into the trees. Somewhere nearby, Tak and Mendy started to bicker, driving Mia to get away. Memorizing what her current spot looked like, she began to wander, climbing over roots and vines and dirtying her dress with damp soil.

Mia stumbled into a clearing where the trees had been cut down to stubs. Wooden planks surrounded an opening in a man-made mound of earth. Mia peered inside, finding a mine shaft, now falling into disuse. Brimming with curiosity, she crawled into the dirty hole, catching her dress on a nail and having to unhook it loose. The shaft of the old ruby mine plunged deep into the earth, with a decrepit wooden cart not far from the entrance, resting on a wooden track falling apart with age. Mia crawled deeper into the tunnel. As much as the mysterious darkness beckoned, she knew that going too far was not a good idea, in case the shaft collapsed or she got lost. Yet every time she told herself to turn back, she just had to take a few more steps.

When the darkness was near complete, a hole in the soil on the side of the tunnel caught Mia's attention. She knelt down and peeked inside, finding a cloth sack. She reached in and pulled it out, shrieking and dropping the sack when a pack of glistening spiders ran out of the hole. Brushing spiders away, Mia picked up the weighty sack, replete with the satisfying clink of coins. Opening it, she also discovered a sheathed, bejeweled dagger and a peculiar wooden rod.

What a lucky discovery. This ought to help Tak and Mendy after the robbery, and make them happy. Excited, Mia clambered back out of the mine shaft, the skirt of her dress now brown with dirt. She rushed back into the trees, searching for the place where they had stopped and hoping she was going in the right direction. Mia had not realized that the sun would go down so soon. Flies and insects buzzed and clung to her sweat-dampened face.

Mia's sharp ears caught Tak and Mendy's voices, yelling as they came closer.

"I can't believe she just ran off!" Tak wailed, sounding panicked. "You know what, Mendy? I think... I think I'm getting attached to the girl."

"You can't do that!" Mendy shouted at her husband.

"But she's friendly, pretty, and a smart lass to boot. I just hope nothing got her."

"Stop it, Tak! Listen to yourself!" Mendy screamed.

"Let's just keep our heads calm and keep looking."

"Hello," Mia called out from the trees. "I'm over here. I have something for you."

"Mia!" Mendy shouted as the couple climbed through the trees and over the high, mossy roots, following the direction of her voice.

"Why in the hell did you run off like that?" Mendy growled once they were reunited. "You gave us a good fright."

"Don't go off like that again," Tak added. "Not any further than to relieve yourself. What were you doing? You're all dirty."

"I found an old mine shaft."

"And you went into it? Where is your brain, girl?" Mendy exclaimed. "Those old mines have heaven-knows-what living inside them. You could fall and get killed. Where's your common sense?"

"I don't know," Mia mumbled, looking down. "But I found this bag. Here. Look."

Enthusiastically, Tak snatched the bag and felt through its contents. "Coins, all right," he said, finally cracking a smile. "Oh, and a dagger! A very nice, bejeweled one!" He lifted the sharp dagger out of its sheath. The jewels embedded in its silver handle glinted in the dimming sunlight.

"And what is this?" Tak wondered as he pulled out the last object, a gnarled stick with a large, angular lavender crystal attached to one end with leather strips.

"A witch's wand!" Mendy gasped. "My wealthy uncle collected curiosities from around the world, and he had one."

"A witch's wand? What in the world would a witch be doing here?"

"Some westerners do like to fool around with these wands. They used to be imported from the east, before the plague. This wand probably has a lot of value now. We could sell it."

"The dagger looks valuable, too. I think I know what this bag was doing in the mine shaft. Some thief stashed his winnings."

"Imagine that. We're stealing from a thief," Mendy chuckled.

Just before the sun went down, they led the horses to a clearing where the trees had been cut down like they were around the old ruby mine, leaving a graveyard of mossy, disintegrating stumps. They decided not to camp too close to the mine shaft itself in case the thief, or thieves, returned. When insects gathered in thick clouds, Tak set up two canvas tents to protect the party from bites. As they ate a quick dinner of dry food around the fire, they talked a bit, Tak and Mendy still in a much improved mood after discovering the coins and valuables.

"I'm sorry if I ran off and startled you earlier," Mia apologized. "I'm just curious, I suppose."

"It's okay," Tak assured her. "Just don't do it again. Especially as we get into ahra territory."

"Is there really such a thing as witches?" Mia wanted to know.

"Why do you ask?"

"You two were saying that the odd stick in that bag is a witch's wand. But I asked my best friend Cady about witches once, and she said that they're just something in fairy stories. Do some people just like to pretend to be witches and make wands?"

"There is indeed such a thing as witches," said Mendy. "I don't know a whole lot about them, just what my uncle told me. They live in the eastern part of the world, in the country of Dorovi, which is just south of Kai'Zi."

It was hard for Mia to get to sleep that night, the air too stuffy in her tent. She tossed and turned, her hair sticking to her face with sweat. Strange creatures wailed and howled from the treetops. In the middle of the night, Mendy screamed and woke everyone. A snake had slithered into the tent she shared with Tak. They threw it outside before it bit anyone.

The next day, after a quick breakfast of stale biscuits, they broke down the camp, keeping their pack of horses as close together as possible just in case today was the day they ventured into ahra land.

"Ugh, what's that smell?" Mendy complained a few hours later, wrinkling her nose as they followed the faint trail.

"Look down," Mia called out from behind her. On the loamy ground, near the horses' hooves, was a vibrant blue blossom, befouling the air with the unmistakable scent of decay.

"Smelly flowers. That's what they warned us about," Tak

reminded them. "Ladies, now is the time that we stick together, even when we relieve ourselves."

The horses were kept practically nose to rump in their line. As they rode along slowly and carefully in the deep shade under the tree canopy, occasionally catching rotten stomach-turning whiffs from the flowers, Mia glanced around nervously in the thick tangle of trees and vines. Occasionally, out of the corner of her eye, a long-armed monkey swung from branch to branch, screeching and howling. Sloths clung to a few trunks. Mia decided that she really didn't like the jungle. Aside from the bugs she constantly had to sweep out of her face, she felt too closed in.

"Do you know how long it's going to take us to get out of this jungle?" Mia asked from her saddle.

"A few days at least," Tak said after unfolding and studying the map. "I'm not sure exactly how much we have ahead of us."

"What's just north of us? Please tell me it'll be plains, or nice cool woods."

"Hmm... looks like it turns to savanna for a bit, then desert. I've let myself lose track of time, but I believe it's around springtime in the north right now, which means the desert will heat up."

"Tak, I'm hot already," Mendy complained. "The inside of my dress feels like a steam bath."

"Well, honey, get ready for more. In the desert it'll be worse. We'd better make sure all of the canteens are full."

"I know what we could do in the desert," Mia suggested. "We could sleep during the day and move at night."

"Now, Mia," Mendy said sternly, "I'm not sure we want to be asleep when everyone else is awake, in case there are any other strange men looking for us. We could be caught by surprise when we're snoozing in our tents."

"People could look for us at night too."

"Ugh, you've always got to... what was that?"

All three of them paused, and even the horses stopped

in their tracks, wide-eyed and snuffling. Far off in the trees, a creature screamed. The screech was cut short as something thrashed violently through the foliage. And then all was still. Too silent. The colorful birds stopped squawking in the trees.

"Let's just keep going," Tak encouraged. "The faster we move, the sooner we'll get out of here."

As they rode along the dim trail, lit only with a few columns of sunlight spilling from above the trees, Mia could not deny that she would need to urinate soon. She pretended the need did not exist until it nagged at her with painful urgency.

"I'm really sorry," she told Tak and Mendy, "but I, uh, need to stop."

"I think we're all needing to do our business," Mendy added.

Mia had never been so scared to walk on the ground before. As soon as the three dismounted from their horses, they huddled close together, finding a small hollow. They gathered in a triangle, all turned away from each other to provide the most privacy possible under the circumstances. This was going to be awkward no matter what. Mia lifted up her dress, face flushing at the bloodstains on her underpants.

"Oh, no, I should have taken a... um... special cloth," she stammered, having forgotten that this was due to happen.

Mendy nodded knowingly. "It's the monthly curse, and it couldn't have come at a worse time. I'm afraid we're going to have to go back to the horses and get some ladies' supplies."

Tak looked like he was on the verge of throwing up. Both he and Mia blushed as her embarrassment ran deep. They ventured to the pack horse to grab a cloth for Mia's underpants, and then stuck together as they returned to the little hollow to finish toileting. Once done, they rushed back to the horses, all three of them mounting at the exact same time.

When it was nearly sundown, they started looking for a place to set up camp. After finding a small, flat clearing with a premade campfire ring, they were just about to hunker down when they made a disturbing discovery—a dropped quiver full of bright-feathered arrows, and nearby, a human skull overgrown with moss, its gray teeth grinning. Right next to the skull, another one of those blue flowers opened its petals, scenting the thick air with the essence of rot. The party wanted to camp somewhere with no dead bodies, but since it would get dark soon, they stayed here, trying unsuccessfully to ignore the smell and forget that the skull existed.

Setting up camp was much less efficient when they had to stay within inches of each other at all times. Yet they got a fire going in the hopes that the bright light would scare away predators, and set up one tent in which they'd all cram themselves. All the close hovering felt too trapping for Mia as they cooked a simple stew from bland dried ingredients. Tak and Mendy got in a fight over whether to add bay leaves or pepper to the stew, how one spice or the other might utterly ruin the flavor, and how Mendy was cutting the potatoes wrong. Mia could not escape into the peaceful sanctuary of the trees this time. She held her head and bit her lip. Mendy hurled a potato across the campsite in frustration, yelling, "Tak, you make everything so hard!"

That night, it just did not feel proper to share a cramped tent with a married couple. Mia snuggled in next to Mendy, against the canvas wall. Just before they went to sleep, Tak, his voice still tense from the argument about the soup ingredients, reminded the ladies that if one of them had to do their business, or if Mia had to change her cloth, they had to wake the other two up so they could all venture outside together.

It was hard to get to sleep. When a breeze blew by and made the tent flap, Mia gasped, thinking for a split second it was an ahra tearing its way in. Finally, she drifted off into jumbled dreams.

The next day, they rode as quickly as possible, limiting their group toileting breaks and scarfing down their lunch fast. They hoped to be out of ahra territory by the end of the day, but found the odorous blue flowers still blooming on the ground as they hunted for another place to set up their camp for the evening. They staked their tent in another small hollow.

Searching for rocks and dry wood for the campfire was much more difficult when they had to cluster together. When the three could do chores separately, setting up camp went much faster, and this became frustrating, especially when an argument brewed over Mendy gathering wood that was too damp to burn. Tak and Mendy staunchly gave each other the silent treatment by the time they nestled into the tent. Mia promised herself that as soon as they were out of reach of the ahras, she would set up her individual tent at the far end of their campsites. These people were increasingly awful to travel with; how nice it would be to enjoy little bits of time to herself again!

After not sleeping well the past few nights, Mia quickly blacked out. She began to dream about the island of her birth. It still had the same volcanic dip in the middle and the same windblown palm trees, but when she ran out barefoot to the beaches, she found them ice-cold and powdery. Instead of their fine-grained sugar sand, the beaches were coated with snow. An ocean of sheer blue ice enclosed the island, rather than the waves of water. When Mia stepped out onto the sheath of ice, it was thick and solid beneath her feet, and she began to slide across the flawless shining surface.

A fine crack appeared just beneath Mia's feet as the ice loudly broke. The thunder of the crack woke Mia up. Her eyes opened to the door of the tent flapping, revealing glimpses of the fire outside, now burned down to glowing red coals.

Mia sat up. Beside her, Mendy lay on her side, snoring. On the opposite side of Mendy, Tak's bedding was flat and empty. His sleepy footsteps thudded outside, further and further away.

Tak was outside. Alone.

Mia shook Mendy, beginning to panic. "Tak stepped out!"

"What?" Mendy mumbled.

"Wake up! Tak left!"

"I'm tired... uh... oh no. Oh no!" Mendy's eyes shot open. Both of them scrambled frantically out of the tent, into the silver moonlight.

Tak shrieked. Something crashed through the brush. His second scream was cut short as Mia and Mendy ran in the direction of the sounds. Tied to nearby trees, the horses whinnied frantically. Out of the corner of Mia's eye, something long and red and pink and gray dashed into the bushes, so fast it was almost completely a blur.

"Tak?" Mendy called, her voice trembling as she clung to Mia's hand. "Tak?"

There was no answer. They anxiously peered around in the glow from the red-hot coals.

"I saw something," Mia said, pointing. "Maybe he's over there."

In their bare feet, they walked to the edge of the clearing. Mia looked down just in time to avoid stepping in a glistening pool of blood, enough that she could smell it. She led Mendy around it and then shuddered to a stop again. Her body tingled and her heart pounded.

There was Tak, lying on the ground partway out of the bushes, his legs splayed. The front of his pants was unfastened. Mia prodded at Tak's leg with her foot, hoping to get a response.

No, it was just part of Tak. His body above the waist was ripped away and missing, leaving only blood-drenched earth and a few entrails.

"Tak!" Mendy cried, seeing the outline of his legs in the darkness and thinking her husband was whole. Before she could crouch down to shake him, Mia held her back with an outstretched arm.

"He's dead, Mendy," Mia warned.

"No!" Mendy screamed, her voice now shrill. "You're lying!"

A gray form darted in front of them. Even though it moved almost too fast to see, Mia caught sight of one horrific feature: long, parted razor-sharp fangs, like those on a man-eating shark. It snatched up the bottom half of Tak's body and disappeared with it into the trees. There was now nothing left of him but fresh blood. Not far off, Mia could hear the excited snarls and gnashing teeth of a feeding frenzy.

Standing there in their nightshirts, clinging to one another, Mia and Mendy broke down and cried. Soon their sobs were the only sound other than the loud song of the insects who came to bite them.

∞ ∞ ∞

In the morning, it rained. Mendy, her eyes bloodshot from her crying, was too distraught to do anything. Mia, using the skills she'd learned from watching Tak, singlehandedly broke down the tent and packed their things as Mendy followed her around like a shadow. The blankets got wet in the rain that drizzled down between the high leaves and vines and curtains of moss, but Mia was beyond caring.

Mendy wanted to leave the site of her husband's grisly death as fast as possible. She mounted the horse that had been Tak's, and briefly glanced at the map that thankfully had been kept dry in his thick leather bag. Ink from the map ran a bit as the raindrops hit it. Numbly, Mendy and Mia set on their way with two riderless horses trailing behind them. They pulled up the hoods on their cloaks, even though their hair was already soaked and stuck to their cheeks.

"I think this is the way," Mendy mumbled in her flat, depressed voice. "Tak was always better at maps than me."

"It does look like we're still on a trail." Mia cleared her throat, nearly at a loss for words. "And there's one of those stone piles right there, marking the way. I'm uh... I'm really sorry about what happened to Tak. I wish I knew of something better to say, but I know nothing is going to make it better."

"Why did he do that? Why did he leave us?"

"His pants were open when I found... the body. I think he needed to pee and was half-asleep, so he forgot about the ahras."

Mendy slumped into a sad mound on Tak's saddle. "I won't have anything of him to bring home with me. Not even his necklace. Now our boys are without a father. I don't know how they are going to handle the bad news when I get back."

"It wasn't easy hearing about it when I found out for sure my parents were dead."

"Yes... I know. I was just remembering how I met Tak. I was about your age. I lived with my mother in the north bank of Dakor City. We were wealthy. I went to a dance social. And there Tak was, with his cousin who lived in town. He was a farm boy from the middle of nowhere who didn't grow up with money, but still so charming and handsome. We eloped but two weeks later. My mother wanted me to marry a rich boy that I hated. When I married Tak instead, she disowned me. Oh, those first months with Tak, before I fell pregnant... it was grand."

"You miss him."

"Of course," Mendy said, lost in rose-tinted memories, sounding fonder of the man than she ever had in Mia's experience while he was still alive. "We spent more of our lives together than apart. It still doesn't feel real, that thanks to this journey, he's not... he's not with us anymore."

"I know. I'm sad too."

Mendy's voice turned cold and stony. "And we're going on this journey because of you. If it weren't for you, I'd still have a husband."

"But I didn't..."

"Shut up!" Mendy snapped. "You worthless young whore! You cost me my Tak!"

Deeply hurt, cut to the bone, Mia sunk her head into her hands and cried as Mendy led the line of four horses in silence. Mia was too afraid to speak up as the day went on and they finally rode out of ahra territory, no longer seeing or smelling the pungent blue flowers. Mia hoped that she was just living in a nightmare. When she woke up, Tak would still be alive and well, he and Mendy might bicker, and then they would pack up camp and leave this same way as the warm sun beat down upon them.

∞ ∞ ∞

The days went by uncomfortably as Mendy took her anger and grief out on Mia. The jungle turned into a grassy marsh, more open to the sunlight, with shorter vegetation. As the evening fell, Mia could see hills coated with deep green rainforest right behind her when she looked over her shoulder, underneath the massive white ring that was now to the south. The top of the great ridged arc looked identical to the bottom that she'd grown up looking at. Mia began to search around for campsites, and asked for input from Mendy.

"Do whatever you want," Mendy growled. "I don't care."

Mia selected a small grassy knoll, a bit higher up and less wet. Mendy pointedly ignored Mia as she set up camp, erecting the tent in case it rained—not a small task for just one person, but a task she was getting pretty good at with a sulking traveling companion who only barely helped. When Mia asked Mendy what she wanted for dinner, Mendy grumpily rolled her eyes and snapped, "I don't care." They just ate bread and cheese, not bothering with a fire as the sun slowly set on the horizon.

"So, um... I know you're upset right now," Mia said gingerly in a quaking voice. "But, Mendy... do you still want to, uh, do this?"

"Do what?"

"Go on this journey."

"Of course, you dimwit. Maybe you got Tak killed, but we still owe it to my boys to get that inheritance. It'd be stupid to turn around after we came this far."

"Mendy, I'm sorry. Really, I am."

"Just shut up! No matter how much you whine, it isn't bringing my husband back." Mendy turned her back on Mia, who started to cry again, and did not speak a word to her for the rest of the evening as they bedded down in the tent.

Mia was used to taking the blame for other people's

unhappiness and burdens. Her parents had ground that shame deep into her, a shame that persisted years after the volcano drowned them in lava and ash. Mia had actually had no control over Tak's failure to wake his two companions when he stumbled out of the tent in a half-asleep stupor, attracting the jungle predators. But she didn't stop for long to think about this. Mia took the terrible, crushing responsibility for Tak's gruesome demise. And for not building a raft big enough for her parents and siblings, or telling them she was leaving the island. She cried herself to sleep.

In the middle of the night, Mia awoke to screams. Shooting upright from the damp bedding, she found herself in an empty tent. Oh, no. It was happening again—the ahras were eating Mendy! Mia grabbed the jewel-handled dagger from the confiscated money bag nearby and dashed out of the tent.

There were human forms bathed in the ruddy glow of torches, walking away from the camp. All of them had great shiny coils of hair piled high on top of their heads, and rings pierced through their noses. Most wore nothing but loincloths on their suntanned bodies, and they spoke to each other, excitedly chattering in a language Mia did not understand. A frantically writhing figure was strapped with rope to a wooden sled pulled through the grass behind the crowd.

Mendy, tied up and gagged.

"Let her go!" Mia screamed, brandishing her dagger. The crowd stopped and turned around, their cold pale eyes glinting in the glow from their handheld torches.

"This lady got good meat on her bones," an old man said with a huge smile, staring Mia down as he gestured toward Mendy. "She fat like pig."

"Meat good and greasy," the young woman next to him agreed. A sling hung around her shoulders, holding a baby. "Stew for days!"

"You young," the man added, eyes locked with Mia's. "Taste better!"

The crowd charged at Mia with long, stone-pointed spears.

Mia kept her dagger raised, shouting. "Go away! Let her go!"

One of the young loincloth-clad men laughed. An elaborate network of scars covered his muscular chest. "We stronger."

Wishing that she'd grabbed Tak's crossbow instead, Mia turned and ran in terror. She raced toward the spot where she had staked the horses, hoping she remembered what bag the crossbow was in.

An arm shot around Mia's neck, choking her. Blind with fear, Mia dropped her dagger. Her hands shot up, fingernails digging into the hard, muscular arm that wouldn't budge. A bundle of grass was shoved into her mouth to muffle her screams as another pair of hands tightly bound her ankles together with rope. Flashing back to memories of childhood beatings with her wrists tied, she fell with a thud into the grass as someone dragged her backwards by the ankles. Mia's hands grabbed clots of dirt as she struggled for something firm to hold onto.

Mia tried to focus her mind, searching hard for a way to spare herself and Mendy from becoming pots of human stew. Without any weapons in hand and unable to get up, her options were limited. But she had to do something, and quick. As the cannibals advanced across the wet marsh, chatting in their native language with the carefree tone people used for talking about the weather, the tent and horses got smaller and smaller.

Mia managed to sit up, and she grasped for the rope that was painfully tight around her ankles. The point of a spear almost pierced her chest as the old man jabbed it toward her heart in warning, forcing her back down to the ground.

Mia's racing thoughts turned toward wishful fantasies. If only ahras lived here in the marsh, and if only they ate people in groups instead of those they caught alone. What she wouldn't give for one of those ravenous creatures to charge toward her captors, giving them a good scare and putting some of them on the bottom of the food chain for once. Right now, it was going to take a miracle. As hard as she wished for a crowd-eating ahra, she knew it was impossible. Mia resigned herself. She and Mendy were doomed.

The surrounding cheery conversation went quiet, and then turned to screams. The rope tying Mia's feet slackened and her ankles fell as the one pulling the rope let go. The group dashed off in all directions, screeching.

"Ahra! Ahra!" cried a woman's terrified voice.

A yell was cut short by the hideous wet sound of tearing flesh. More screams erupted all around as the crowd scattered.

Mia propped herself up as a gray wolfish form, a blur just like the ones that laid waste to Tak, zipped back and forth. The survivors ran as fast as they could into the distance, dropping their spears and torches and wailing in horror. The ahra faded until it vanished into the moonlight. There was no sound but Mendy's moaning through the grass that filled her mouth, and the crying of an infant.

Mia untied her ankles and undid the cloth gag around her head, and then dashed back to the campsite. When she found the dagger lying in the grass, she returned to Mendy, still tied to the abandoned wooden sled, and sawed through the ropes that held her body down. When she slashed the cloth around Mendy's head, Mendy sat up and spat out the grass, scowling. "What in the hell just happened?"

"I haven't the faintest idea. But we're safe now."

"That child screaming over there. Go find its mother, shut it up, or something."

Mia went looking for the wailing baby and spotted it wriggling in the grass, surrounded by a gory scene of destruction—great pools and smears of blood, disembodied arms and legs. Mia carefully picked her way across the sticky ground toward the infant. It was still in its woven sling, now stained with red. She gathered the baby, sling and all, into her arms. Mendy followed her as she walked in silence back to the camp, thankful to be alive yet saddened that the baby, at its mother's breast just moments ago, was probably now an orphan.

"I don't want to deal with a damned baby," Mendy

grumbled as they climbed back into the tent.

"What do you want me to do, leave it here to starve?"

"If we don't find a wet nurse, it'll starve anyway."

"Can't we find a way to feed this child?"

"You idiot. Have you given birth?"

"I thought you knew I don't have children."

"I was being sarcastic, dimwit! You don't produce mother's milk. And mine dried up years ago. Thanks to you, we get to take this baby with us and watch it starve."

"Mendy, I don't know what to tell you, but at least our flesh isn't being cut from our bones and tossed into pots of stew. Even though what happened to those people was utterly frightening. I don't know if that was an ahra, or what it could have been. I thought ahras didn't live here or attack groups. It doesn't make sense." Mia began to cry, unable to ignore that the maulings coincided with her wishful thinking about ahras. Was she to blame? Like she was for everything else?

"Just get us out of here," Mendy sighed. "The sun's not up yet, but I cannot sleep after all that."

Mia was left with the chore of breaking down the tent by the light of a torch and packing it away as Mendy sat and glowered. Mia put the sling holding the heavy warm baby around her shoulders. The infant fell asleep against Mia's chest, soothed by her heartbeat. Mia checked the map, and then they set on their way before dawn. As they rode, Mendy stayed silent while Mia felt sick to her stomach, the series of bloody recent events flashing before her eyes over and over. She didn't know how she was going to sleep again for a week at least. These wilds held too many dangers.

After the sun came up, Mia was tired but didn't want to stop anytime soon, not knowing what other predators, human or otherwise, might be too close by. She assumed Mendy wanted to keep going for the day as well, but couldn't be sure, as Mendy no longer responded to her. When the baby woke in its sling and started crying, Mia noticed that the woven grass diaper was wet.

"Mendy," Mia said, "the child has a dirty diaper."

Still stony and silent, Mendy stopped her horse, and the line halted.

"You're the one who has raised children," Mia continued. "What do you suppose I use for a diaper?"

"Just use whatever," Mendy snapped. "I don't care."

Mia dismounted her horse, still wearing the baby on her chest. She removed the infant from the sling and pulled off the woven diaper, noticing that the child was a female. Not certain of what else to do, Mia took one of her hygiene cloths from her saddlebag and stuffed it between the baby's chubby legs, hoping it would suffice. When the baby failed to stop crying, Mia figured she was hungry, so she grabbed her canteen and dripped water between the plump little lips. The thirsty infant got angrier, then finally gave in and sipped a few drops.

As they rode on, Mia's skin got uncomfortably hot, inappropriately so even in the balmy humid weather. She attributed it to exhaustion and the considerable recent trauma that she and Mendy had endured. Mendy slumped more than usual in Tak's saddle, probably crushed under her overpowering grief and her lack of sleep.

"Look over there," Mia pointed. "A town."

Mendy's head turned toward the cluster of black stone ziggurats on the horizon.

"What I wouldn't do for a nice bed," Mendy said quietly, her voice softening into an almost friendly tone.

They beelined for the village, mostly quiet except for a few ruby merchants in the streets. With the money found in the mine shaft, they got a room at the inn. The food in the torchlit dining hall was not particularly appetizing, too greasy, but Mia festooned her meat and mashed potatoes with a few death pepper seeds to add flavor. Like an answer to a prayer, a nursing mother happened to be dining nearby. She agreed to feed the restless orphaned baby as soon as she learned of Mia and Mendy's situation.

"Would you be willing to take on this child?" Mia asked as the baby happily suckled, the woman rocking her in her arms.

"I have my hands full, I'm afraid. I have twin boys and my three-month-old babe. I'll still be here in the morning and can provide a few more feedings, but after that, you might want to hire a wet nurse or find yourself a goat."

Mendy acted moody, smoldering with anger again, when she and Mia went to bed. The innkeepers gave them a small straw-lined basket for the infant to sleep in. Mendy laid down in her bed and turned toward the wall.

"Uh, Mendy," Mia asked carefully. "I have a question."

"What are you bothering me for now?"

"With all due respect, you seem very unhappy with me and there seems to be nothing I can do to make it right. Would it be easier for us if we, er... split up? If I go back to Dakoris and you go on to Loriar?"

"You're not going back to Dakoris," Mendy said harshly.

"But would you rather be alone?"

"No. I need you with me. So we... can both... collect the inheritance." Mendy started to cough, a troubling rattle coming from deep in her chest.

"You okay? Are you choking?"

"No, just hay fever. Now do me a favor and leave me alone."

Mia had trouble getting to sleep; her feverish body began to ache all over. She tossed and turned; even when she threw the blankets off, the bed roasted her like an oven. She blamed her discomfort on the humid climate and all the recent stress.

Though she gave thought to the events as she tossed restlessly in bed, Mia could not figure out what had happened to the band of cannibals the night before. Surely it couldn't have been an ahra that killed them, targeting a group for once. It came seemingly at Mia's will, obeying the call of her mind. No, it couldn't have been because of her. How could her thoughts, unspoken, lure a deadly wild beast out of its range to engage in unnatural behavior? Was there some other species, a cousin of the ahra?

And if that beast had such an appetite for blood, why did it spare Mia, Mendy, and the baby?

When they woke in the morning, Mia's joints screamed in pain. Even though Mendy ignored Mia's complaints, Mia could tell by her shuffle and her groans that she was sore, too. Even so, they ate breakfast, had the kind young mother nurse the baby again, and left.

After losing her husband and almost losing her own life, Mendy decided to travel the main highway at least for a while, taking the risk of being followed. She preferred all the traffic and the safety in numbers to the dangers out in the wilds. And this gave them a much greater chance of getting help for the infant. Mendy advised Mia to keep her cloak hood drawn up and her eyes down as they rode. They kept to the middle of a cluster of travelers coasting along on horses and in oxen-pulled carts.

Mia felt worse and worse. She began to cough, a deep, rheumy hacking from low in her lungs. Later, Mia looked up and noticed Mendy swaying from side to side in her saddle, struggling to hold her head up.

"Mendy! Are you okay?" Mia shouted, triggering herself into a coughing fit. The baby started to fuss in the sling.

There was no response. Just a hacking cough.

"You ladies don't look good at all," a nearby trader observed, peering at them with concerned eyes from his oxen-drawn carriage. He raised his voice, attracting the attention of other travelers nearby. "Hello, these girls need help. They're ill and they have a babe with them. Does anybody know the way to the nearest healer?"

Another man steered his white horse toward Mendy and Mia. "You need a healer?"

"I think we do," Mia said weakly. "I think we're sick."

"Did you just come out of the marshes by the jungle?"

"Yes."

"If this is what I think it is... I know of someone in the next village. Be glad that Parem has some of the best healers in the world. Right now, I think you'll need all the luck you can get. Follow me."

Mia and Mendy could barely muster the strength to sit

upright in their saddles when they reached the village, a circle of small ziggurats rising from the grassy savanna. The man led the line of horses to one sprawling property with a round house made from the same black stones that composed most Parem architecture, and knocked on the door. A short, squat old woman, weighed down with brass jewelry and elaborate beaded hair, answered.

"Ehria says to come inside right away," the man instructed Mia and Mendy. "Don't come near me; I don't want to catch it. I'll hitch your horses for you, and then I'll be on my way."

Mia almost fell as she got out of the saddle. Still balancing the baby in the sling, she staggered into the round house, Mendy following close behind. The inside of the circular home was lined with wooden shelves of jars and bowls stuffed with herbs. Pallets were scattered on the floor—sickbeds. One of those beds held a delirious child who appeared to have a couple of broken bones, wrapped tightly with medicine-soaked strips of cloth. Mia thought of her oldest sister, Lata, who broke her leg and then died from fever. Mia had a fever now. Was she doomed?

Ehria, the old healer, circled around Mia and Mendy, patting their foreheads and pinching their arms, asking them to sit down to catch their breath.

"You came from the marshes just north of the jungle?"

"We went through them, yes," Mia told her in a raspy voice.

"You have the wetland plague. Must have been bit by the wrong mosquitoes. It gets worse before it gets better. Is your baby sick?"

"No, I don't think so. And this isn't my child." She explained what had happened as the healer plucked the sleepy baby from the sling.

"Ahhh. I am not too worried about the baby. Those cannibals don't catch the plague. Their bodies must be resistant to disease. Maybe human flesh is their secret; too bad I can't stomach the thought of it, 'else I might live to be a hundred and twenty. Very strange about the ahra though; that shouldn't have happened."

"I don't think... we can... take care of her." Mia leaned forward, propping herself on her knees as she got out of breath in a hacking fit.

"Both of you go lie down immediately, in those pallets over there. I'll find a place for the baby."

After Mia and Mendy bedded down into the straw-lined pallets, Ehria washed the infant in a basin and fed her some sort of milk with herbs from a cup. And then she got to work on her woodstove, stirring something smelly in a pot. The mixture was still steaming when she brought two wooden bowls to Mendy and Mia, instructing them to drink the foul potion in its entirety. Immediately afterward, they both fell asleep. Mia's dreams were vivid and disturbing and nonsensical, filled with blood and sand and snow.

It was broad daylight when she opened her eyes again. She felt chained to the floor, completely drained of energy. Next to her, Mendy still slept, mumbling, each raspy breath rattling with congestion. The healer was at the stove again.

"You're awake, very good," Ehria told Mia when she turned around and noticed her open eyes, handing her a ceramic cup with another odorous medicinal mixture. It tasted bitter, metallic. Mia gagged.

"Loriki grass root and blood of the ox. Drink up to get your strength back."

Mia sipped at the disgusting drink floating with brown blood clots, gagging it down. "Where's... the... baby?" she gasped.

"Don't you worry about the baby. My daughter took her in. She's feeding her milk from her goat. You just worry about getting better."

"Will your daughter... keep her?"

"Yes. She is very kind-hearted and this is not the first orphan she's taken in. The child will know she's not of our race, but she doesn't have to know she was born of the cannibals."

"Will I get... better?" Mia gasped. "Will I... die?"

"Do you want an honest answer?"

"Yes."

"With my healing medicine, it's about a fifty-fifty chance. But with no medicine, about eight out of ten will die. I'm giving you the best chance I can."

"Am... I... at... the worst part?"

"No. I'll give you medicine to keep you asleep. Your companion is sicker than you. I've already put her to sleep."

As she lay ill in the pallet, Mia's world became fuzzier and fuzzier, blacker and blacker, and time was seemingly suspended. She slept more and more, her few waking hours plagued by her painful rattling cough. She used what little energy she had to consume tiny bits of soup and drink the healer brought to her lips for nourishment. Because she sweated from the fever and did not have much energy to wash herself, Mia was only dimly aware of the healer occasionally pulling her dress away and wiping her skin down with soap and a wet cloth, and placing a shallow pot beneath her bottom.

Helplessly, after gulping down some especially bitter medicine spooned to her mouth, Mia drifted off until her entire life became a dream. Blackness, visions, and then more blackness surrounded her. Her parents and siblings, even Lata who'd been dead since Mia was six, came back to life, running around the island, happier than they'd ever been, playing tag in the palm trees. Mia's brother Deto left her alone except for one apologetic hug, and even her sister Sireh smiled at and spoke to her. Mia was dismayed to be right back where she started, yet relieved to be out of this world full of cannibals and ahras and deadly diseases. Back in that safe enclave, now with a much kinder family too. Mia wondered if the fever had killed her and the island with this happier revived family was her own personal heaven. This wasn't like the heaven they talked about in Dakoris, where reborn sheep roamed happily on the fleecy ring in the sky under the gentle direction of the sheep-goddess.

The beaches were covered in snow like they had been in a few past dreams, soft and glittering in the sun. It swished, powdery, around Mia's bare feet, and the ocean of ice extended all around. Curious, Mia walked across the ice, which this time didn't crack. She came upon another mound of snow, dotted with tall pointed evergreen trees. A marble building with turrets on the edges rose out of the trees. So did a few smaller wooden houses with roofs that slanted all the way down to the ground on one side. A huge waving green-blue curtain streaked across the darkened sky, casting a faint green glow upon these unusual houses. It was the most beautiful thing Mia had ever seen, this bright, colorful shimmer undulating in the night sky. She'd heard of these sky-lights, which put on their nightly show over the southernmost mountains and glaciers of Dakoris, where only a few tough souls lived. But she had never seen it. Not until now. The ring around the earth was a small whiteness on the horizon.

The visions got more jumbled after that, a nonsensical blur of memories, faces, sensations, and sounds. Mia saw herself a little older and dressed up in glamorous clothing she'd never worn before, the self she had looked upon in dreams as a child, playing the harp as long silver-white hair in its natural color swept around her shoulders like a waterfall. There was a man too, tall and wrapped in a handsome robe made of furs, face clean-shaven. That same long dazzling silvery hair cascaded beneath a jeweled circlet around his head. A male version of Mia?

It all slowly fell apart and revealed Ehria's house, dim and gauzy and too quiet inside. Outside the open window, something burned, an animal roasting over a spit perhaps. A hint of charred flesh scented the air. Tired and sore from being flat on her back, Mia weakly reached over and turned her head to the empty pallet next to her. Where was Mendy? The child with the broken bones, who'd been lying bandaged up when Mia and Mendy first arrived sick and feverish, was also gone.

The blackness came and, with it, another strange dream of those iridescent lights in the sky. A dream that seemed so real it had Mia thinking she had died and gone to heaven.

∞ ∞ ∞

"Take it easy," said Ehria's voice as Mia's eyes, nearly crusted shut, opened slowly and painfully. A small cup was tipped to her lips, filled with a lemony tea. "There, there. Wonderful. You pulled through great."

Mia struggled to sit up. Some of her muscles, weak from disuse, screamed from the strain as she propped herself up on her arms.

"Easy, easy. You need to get your strength back. Drink up."

Mia sipped down the rest of the steaming tea. The healer took the cup away, explaining that she wanted to keep Mia for a few more days to recuperate before she went anywhere.

Mia turned her head to Mendy's pallet, once again finding it empty. So maybe it was not a dream the last time Mia had briefly awoken to find herself alone in the house. Mendy must have already gotten better and now was waiting on Mia, or perhaps she had become fed up and decided to venture to Loriar on her own. What would Mia do if she'd been left behind, with no horses or money?

"Mendy left without me?" Mia asked. She sounded like the walking dead, her throat caked with old congestion.

Ehria lowered her head. "No, she..."

Just then, a man burst into the house, shouting and out of breath. "Ehria! Ehria! Can you please come help us? My wife is in labor and something's gone wrong! The midwife doesn't know what to do!"

"I'll be back as soon as I can," Ehria assured Mia. "Rest until I return."

When the healer left, Mia found herself completely alone. Even though her legs creaked like rusted metal, she managed to get herself up to a wobbly standing position. She peeked around the exhaustive collection of herbs and the cubbyholes below the shelves, where she found the bag from the mine shaft with the coins, dagger, and wand. She also discovered her fake identification papers with the name Nori Tethlo. Mia could not remember if Ehria had even asked for her name.

Mia's stomach constricted with extreme hunger. She had to go lie back down, and she stared up at the ceiling. It was made of wood spokes radiating out from the center, and it almost appeared to spin.

Where was Mendy?

Later, Ehria returned, looking frazzled. She immediately set to work cooking a dinner for Mia. She handed her a plate of grilled meat and vegetables, and went out black and cut the throat of a frantically bleating young calf in her stable of animals. She returned with a cup of salty calf's blood with herbs mixed in.

"Eat and drink as much as you can. For your strength."

Even though it was freshly drained and not clotted, Mia found the blood fairly disgusting with its iron taste. But in her starving hunger, she almost didn't care. These Parem people sure seemed fond of blood as a healing agent. It was, after all, a rabbit's blood tonic that had cured the terrible, widespread plague years ago. As Mia choked the drink down with her dinner, Ehria returned to her yard to finish butchering the calf, and then hung the strips of meat over the fire pit.

"You were going to tell me where Mendy is?" Mia asked later, dreading the answer.

"I have some difficult news. I did everything I could. But your friend passed away. There was nothing more I could do for her; she was too sick and had pneumonia as well."

"Oh, no!" Mia clapped her hand to her mouth, tears gathering in her eyes. She and Mendy had not gotten along recently, but now, she was all alone. "We already lost her husband; he was killed by an ahra in the jungle. She has four children that they left at home. Those boys are orphans now and they don't even know it!"

"That is a pity. Those poor boys. Will they have someone to take care of them?"

"A couple are old enough to take care of themselves, and they have an aunt living down the road to help out. Though I guess their mother and father aren't coming back now." Mia sighed sadly. "What was done with Mendy's body? Is she buried somewhere?"

"I had to burn the corpse to keep the disease from spreading. I'm very sorry... Nori, that's your name, correct?"

"Uh... correct."

"Nori, I don't ask questions of the people who come through here. So that's the last question I'll ask of you. Wherever you're heading, or whether you decide to turn back after these terrible losses, is your concern, not mine. I saved something for you to remember your friend by." From a drawer, Ehria produced Mendy's necklace. The pendant was a small clay rendering of the Dakor sheep-goddess.

In the next few days, Mia ate more and more and walked to exercise her weakened muscles. She discovered that she had been bedridden for not just days, but a couple of weeks.

Mia thought about what to do, now the sole survivor of her party. Should she go on alone to Loriar? That was still such a long way—wouldn't it be dangerous, since Tak and Mendy hadn't made it out of Parem alive? But since Danli had cast Mia from her home and Mia had nowhere else to go, no one else to turn to, what did she have to lose? If Mia's journey was successful and she collected the inheritance in Loriar, then she could bring it back for Tak and Mendy's orphaned children to live on. And possibly even keep part of it, too.

Unsure where exactly in Loriar they were going, Mia studied the water-stained map where Tak had drawn the routes they would take, obscure off-the-beaten-path trails when possible. Mia still had quite a distance to cover. The destination was the capital city of Beriniat in the eastern part of Loriar. Tak had said something about collecting the inheritance at the royal palace. Mia decided to set her sights on it. She wasn't sure if it was a good idea to continue, yet this journey had an inexplicable feeling of destiny and purpose that went beyond any bags of money she might earn. This was how she was meant to see the world, fulfilling the goal she had set when she was twelve.

It just was not meant to be so traumatic, both of her companions dead before they even reached Loriar.

When Ehria deemed Mia strong enough to leave, Mia thanked her for saving her life and also asked if she could quickly redo her black hair dye job before stepping out, as the light silver roots had grown in, obvious above the black strands.

"I won't ask you any questions," Ehria reiterated with a knowing look in her eyes.

Danli had urged Mia to hide her features, such as her hair color underneath the dye. When washing Mia's helpless, unconscious bare body at the height of her illness, it was quite likely the healer had spotted glimpses of the silver body hair usually concealed under clothing. When Ehria flipped her over to wipe down her back, what about that odd, perfectly symmetrical birthmark that had somehow sent Danli into such a panic? What would happen now that Ehria had probably noticed it? Would more people be on Mia's tail as she traveled?

When she healed enough to leave, Mia consolidated her, Tak's, and Mendy's belongings into a few bags, making sure to pack Mendy's necklace to give to her sons when she returned to Dakoris with the inheritance. The next thing Mia did before leaving the village was sell two of the horses. It was a bit difficult to part with them after bonding on the trails, but they might be happier at a new home, relaxing in a green pasture. Now that Mia was a party of one, she didn't need four horses. Mia finally left, overwhelmed by the sunlight after weeks spent indoors recuperating. She departed from the town on the horse that she originally rode when she set out from that farm in the middle of Dakoris with Tak and Mendy, with the pack horse trailing behind her.

Not many people surrounded Mia on the road out of town. To pass the time, Mia talked out loud to Mendy, in case her spirit listened.

"It's really too bad that you died angry at me, Mendy. I

hope you will forgive me and find peace in your spirit form, off to pasture with the sheep-goddess. I don't know if you were still angry at me right before you passed, or if you were too sick to know who I was. I was delirious. I barely remember it now; but I saw some very interesting things. I don't remember your last moments. I just hope that you weren't in too much pain when you went. Probably not; Ehria knew how to cook up some medicine that could really knock a person out. I'm so sorry, Mendy, that you won't live to see your boys get the inheritance. But I'll see to it that they'll live comfortably, though there's no way to replace you and their father. And once I'm back at your house and that's all taken care of, I'm afraid I'll have to depart, though where I'll go I don't know, since I'm not welcome at Danli's house anymore. I never wanted to say this out loud to you while you were still alive, but that oldest son of yours was too much like my brother with his wandering hands. I didn't like it one bit."

Afraid of getting lost, and intimidated at the prospect of journeying alone with no one to help her, Mia decided to ride on the main highway for a while. That first evening, she camped in a thicket of trees near the highway. She decided to set up the tent, just in case. Though she was gaining her strength back day by day, she was still exhausted and her muscles a bit weak. Putting together the camp left her rather winded and needing to catch her breath. The second night of her now-solo journey, Mia stayed at a small-town inn. Chronically hungry, she filled up with stew until she was about to burst.

The next day, Mia decided to stop for lunch, perching on a large rock in the hot, dry, flat savanna. As she watched the traffic of feet and hooves and wooden wheels on the main highway, Mia spotted a figure amid the large kicked-up clouds of dust—a woman on a horse, wearing a plain gray short-sleeved Dakor summer cloak, very similar to the one Mia wore. Her hood hung down around her shoulders. Her pale hair was pulled back into a bun, and Mia could not get a good look at the exact hair color, but it may have been blond, gray, or a blend of the two. Dakor travelers were an increasingly rare sight this far north in Parem. Yet this tall, thin woman looked familiar. Too familiar, in fact.

Could that be Danli? The one who had taken Mia in and cared for her, taught her the ways of shepherds and how to spin wool, and given her years of peaceful happiness before suddenly becoming skittish and sending her away?

Despite being angry at the woman for abandoning her, even if she did it out of fear, Mia was almost tempted to run to the woman and draw her attention in case it really was Danli. No, it couldn't be her. What would Danli be doing here? Danli never strayed too far from home, for she found it important to care for her homestead and land with her own hands whenever possible. That lady trudging along on her horse was probably just one of those wool traders who crawled long distances to peddle their wares.

A gray horse trotted along behind the woman's horse, and another cloaked figure sat in the saddle, this one a bit shorter with a slight youthful roundness to her figure and two thick golden braids hanging down her shoulders. Mia could not get a good look at her face but imagined it as Cady, trailing behind Danli. No, that was impossible. Cady wouldn't be here—she was back home. Maybe her and Thom's wedding had already taken place, and they were honeymooning or enjoying their newlywed bliss, leaving Mia in the past.

The two Dakors had passed and disappeared ahead by the time Mia was finished eating her small lunch. Mia carefully rationed the dry food in the packs, and her stomach was still growling when she finished. After she got back on the highway, she began to feel more and more of a sense of being followed again, and not in a good way. Her skin crawled. Even though no one tailed her or acted suspicious, Mia decided to take the risk of a less-traveled path. After asking a couple of merchants for directions and checking the map, she located one of the more obscure northward trails.

"Be careful, lady," a grizzled old merchant warned before Mia veered off onto the thinner trail. "You'll be coming up on the desert. It's early summer and it'll be hotter than the pit of hell. You sure you want to do this?"

"I've already been through enough," Mia said, feeling cynical. "If that desert is going to be the death of me, then so be it."

"All right, then, if you want to play with fate. If you run out of water, you can cut open and drink the juices from the short, fat sort of cactus. The taller ones are poisonous. And you may burn away the spines from the fruit and eat it."

"Thank you."

"When—if—you make it to Loriar, you're in for a shock. You came here from Dakoris, right?"

"Yes."

"Here in the lower countries, we're good to our women. But up in Loriar, as a pretty girl traveling alone, you should be careful. Loriar folks think women are good for nothing except birthing babies and scrubbing floors. I'd keep a dagger handy at all times in case a man tries to... take advantage."

"Thanks for warning me. I don't plan to stay there any longer than I have to. Once I get that money in Beriniat, I'm bringing it back to Dakoris if I make it back alive."

"You've got quite a bit of journeying ahead of you. Loriar's a big country and Beriniat's in the east. Most of the folks from Loriar that I've met are about as backwards as the beasts of the field. Their slaves are smarter than they are."

"The Loriar people keep slaves?"

"The rich ones do, especially the ones running the gold mines. The wealthy men have usually got two families. One with their wife, one with their prettiest slave girl. Now you know what sorts of people you're in for. I wish you all the best."

As Mia traveled on the little-known, little-traveled path, the landscape changed. Stunning spires and wind-carved arches of red sandstone began to rise from the increasingly hilly earth. When the wind blew, it carried bursts of red sand with it. In the baking hot weather, Mia constantly thirsted for water, but she carefully conserved it, giving more of it to the horses than to herself—dead horses would slow her down considerably. She let them stop and graze at every patch of grass that came up.

After a couple of days in the desert, Mia gave up on dealing with the oppressive dry heat that seemed to suck the very life out of her and decided to move at night instead, as she had once suggested to Tak and Mendy while they were still alive. During the day, Mia slept, getting hot and sticky even in the shade of the tent, and kept the horses tied deep in the shadiest spots she could find below shelves of sandstone. After sundown, she relied on the light reflecting from the moon and the great ring to cross the landscape. The purple sky filled with brilliant twinkling stars and the temperature dropped drastically, until it was almost cold. The desert truly was a place of extremes. The horses seemed much happier and less sluggish in the chillier temperatures as they traversed the hills and dunes of cacti-dotted red sand, leaving shadowed trails of hoofprints behind in the celestial light.

Mia had a lot of time to herself to think. She had lost track of what week or even month she was in, but if it was late spring or early summer here, then the fall or early winter season was well along in Dakoris below the equator of jungles. Her birth month might have already passed. She was likely eighteen years old now.

Though it hurt her heart to even think about, Mia contemplated if she was as responsible for Mendy's death as much as Mendy blamed her for Tak's. She knew by now that it didn't make sense—it was the couple's idea to go on this long trip, not Mia's. Just as it was their choice to bring her and leave their children behind. Did they think that Mia had more maturity and could better assist them?

Mia tried to reassure herself that both deaths were truly unfortunate accidents. She had not seen either coming. Still, she was all mixed up and guilty inside.

The trail went on—what Mia thought was the trail. For two nights, she kept on diligently trekking until, one early morning when the sun was tinting the horizon lavender over the sandstone formations, it occurred to Mia that she hadn't seen one of the piled rock cairns that marked the way in days. Instead, she stumbled across a human skeleton half-buried in the windblown sand, ribs arching up and bleached clean from the sun. Panic shot through Mia's body. She was lost. Not only that, but running a bit low on food and nearly out of water, with no rivers or lakes in sight. In her current situation, she would become another long-forgotten skeleton in the sand. This was it. The end of the road.

Instead of bedding down for the day, Mia turned around in a frenzy, following the hoofprints her horses had previously left in the sand and ignoring her exhaustion, wanting to get back on track as quickly as possible. She fell asleep in the shade underneath a red rock outcropping at high noon, sweating and parched.

The wind blew, making the tracks shallower and shallower. On the second night of backtracking, Mia ran out of water and grew desperately thirsty. She sat down, trying to think of the next step. There were plants growing here, plenty of them—cacti, low green agaves, grass. In order for plants to grow, there had to be water somewhere, and there had to be some inside the plants too. Mia followed the advice the merchant gave her and cut down a short, squat cactus, rending the flesh apart. She held the juicy wet innards up to her mouth and chewed and sucked. The fluid tasted very green, not the same as pure water, but still some badly needed refreshment. Mia gave some to the horses.

At last, Mia was back on the correct path, still parched and desperately drawing what little water she could from the plants around her. She rode until dawn, when, miraculously, she encountered a traveler on a white stallion, a man with great ropes of beaded braids dangling from his head to his waist.

"Sir?" Mia asked. "Could you perhaps spare some food and water?"

"You're out?"

"Of water, yes."

Kindly, the stranger offered Mia a full canteen. She drank half of it and put the other half in a bowl for the horses. The man also offered her some dried jerky and cheese, which she gobbled up.

"Where are you going?" he asked.

"I'm heading up to Loriar."

"First, I presume you're going through Parem City?"

"That city on the border? I think so."

"It's a good idea. There's a small village up ahead, and after that, there's not many people until you get to the city."

"After I cross the border to Loriar, will it still be desert?"

"For a while, yes. Much of Loriar is forest, though. Cold in the winter, but I think you will find it refreshing compared to this desert. Say, girl... what's your name?"

"Um... Nori."

"Nori, by any chance, have you seen any young ladies with silver hair? Not an old gray-haired woman, but a young one."

"Silver hair?" An ominous chill trickled through Mia's body. "No, I haven't. Why do you ask?"

"There is a Loriar man to the south of us, looking for a girl of that description. He wanted me to spread the word. Anyway, I've got rubies to sell in Parem City. I'd best be on my way."

Mia trembled with worry after the stranger rode off, his back to the rising sun. There was another man following her now. Her gut feeling had been correct. Mia decided to set up a camp far, far from the trail, in spite of her dyed hair, and rode over stones whenever possible so the tracks wouldn't be so easily visible. She erected the tent on the other side of a tall skinny column of sandstone and devoured the last of her bread before going to sleep.

A village cropped up on the western horizon the next night, an oasis Mia was delighted to see. Instead of Parem's typical ziggurat architecture, this settlement was a clump of red-gold squares leaning up against a tall layered cliff. As she came closer, it became apparent that all of the buildings had been carved straight from the sandstone. They blended in well with the strangely pretty landscape. Mia waited for the sun to come up and for businesses to open, and then she rented a room at the inn, keeping a cautious eye out for any Loriar soldiers. Most of the furniture consisted of slabs hand-rendered from sandstone, including the block where Mia slept on top of a down-filled cushion. An array of sweating, water-filled clay jars somehow kept the building cool.

After waking up in the evening, Mia purchased bread, cheese, salt pork, and cactus fruit from a food stand. She refilled her canteens with well water, took a very welcome and refreshing bath at the inn, and then set out on her way, not wanting to stay in any one place for too long with the knowledge of at least one man looking for her.

As she traveled under the wide sky of bright stars and streaked galaxies and the ever-present ring, Mia found a certain comfort and routine in her complete solitude. Her mind wandered as she rode. When she stopped for breaks, Mia practiced her keen hunting skills, shooting at nocturnal creatures with Tak's crossbow. When she got a jackrabbit, she built a small fire and skewered the skinned animal on a twig, just as she and her family had done with tarniks while she was growing up on the island. The meat was a bit stringy and gamey, but better than nothing, and would help her stretch the supply of food she'd purchased. Cooked and raw cactus and agave flesh were also on the menu, to help conserve the water supply.

∞ ∞ ∞

Parem City, a larger-scale version of the sandstone village Mia had stayed in earlier, was nothing short of stunning, even in the middle of the night when Mia approached. Ringed with an oasis of palm trees, the huge city edged a majestic cliff and sat near a wide, glistening lake and a river that cut across the desert. There were sandstone houses both big and small, with smooth rounded doorways. This city was not asleep, not completely. Light spilled from a few windows.

The inn that Mia found was full. Hungry and thirsty, she came across a local tavern. Deciding to indulge for once, she hitched the horses outside and carried the sack of her most important belongings with her so that it would not get stolen. A long, carved sandstone bench ran around the perimeter of the inside, behind the tables. Mia bought herself some pepper stew and a tankard of bubbling ale. She sat at a table next to a pair of colorfully robed middle-aged gentlemen with salt-and-pepper hair worn long and tied back. They each turned to Mia with a smile and introduced themselves as Davern, a professor who taught history at the University of Parem in the city center, and Rodrik, who fixed houses for a living. Though neither of these men asked about any silver-haired girls, just to be on the safe side, Mia told them her name was Nori. As the small talk continued, they grew increasingly friendly, and Mia couldn't be certain if they were flirting with her or not.

"Have you been in the desert for some time?" Davern the professor asked.

"Yes. I came up from Dakoris."

"I was wondering why you're dressed in Dakor wool, which looks a bit hot for the climate, even with those shorter sleeves. Impressive that you have come all this way on your own. You're a brave soul."

"I didn't start out on my own. I nearly died of an illness before I even reached the desert, and both of my traveling companions died terrible deaths."

"Oh, my goodness. What a rough journey you have had. How have you been braving the heat?"

"I've been moving at night. But still, it has been tough, and I got lost once."

"That's very good thinking and I am thankful that you

found the path again. Many of the travelers, especially at this time of year, don't survive the journey."

"Yes, I saw someone's bones half-buried in the sand."

"In the winter, believe it or not, it's the cold that gets you. The nights can even get freezing. But we are hardy people."

"Where are you heading, Nori?" Rodrik asked.

"To Loriar."

"You're almost there. Is that where you're from originally?"

"No. Well, it's a long story." Mia remembered being told she had a Loriar accent after her rescue from the ocean.

"Long story? I want to hear it! The longer a story, the more interesting."

Mia regaled the two men with her tale about the island. They couldn't imagine growing up so cut off from the rest of the world.

"It does sound like your family was originally from Loriar," Rodrik commented.

"The harsh discipline fits the picture of a Loriar family," Davern added. "The folks there are quite stern, and severe punishments toward wives and children are common. According to my research, things really changed in Loriar over the past four hundred years or so. They used to be happy people, partiers who enjoyed life. The average citizen had an assortment of husbands or wives and other lovers on the side. Homosexuality was accepted back then. And in today's Loriar, it is punishable by death."

Rodrik snickered. "Rampant lovemaking at every turn... it doesn't sound like the worst thing in the world to me. I wonder why they put a stop to that! Now they're all about misery."

"Just curious," said Mia, "in the past, did these people ever get jealous of each other when they had these various lovers?"

"I don't imagine they did," the professor stated. "That was normal for them in those days. It took one ruler, a twisted and bitter king, to change things drastically. According to one of my history books, about four centuries ago, King Eldorat took the throne. When this king was a young man, he courted a very cruel girl who tied him up and threatened to cut off a certain piece of his body that is very important to men. It shook him so badly that he hated women forever after. Once Eldorat inherited the throne, he took out his anger on the entire female sex, and started a whole movement of the men he influenced. They drafted new laws and ordered executions of women. They banned the worship of the goddess that the people of Loriar had worshiped for eons, and permitted only a male god in their new churches. Folks caught flaunting their nudity, practicing homosexuality, or carrying goddess symbols got sent to the torture chambers. And most of Eldorat's successors haven't been much kinder."

"Ugh. Torture chambers!" Mia gasped. "Does that sort of nonsense still go on?"

"Oh, yes. It depends on how sadistic the current king is. Since the time of Eldorat, the rulers of Loriar and their subordinates have also been partial to public hangings, public floggings, public beheadings, and general public humiliation."

"I think the hunger for wealth has bent those people's minds, too," Rodrik added. "They weren't as preoccupied with their gold mines back in the days when they partied and drank and made the beast with two backs, were they?"

"Not particularly," said the professor. "King Eldorat raised the gold production quotas, and so has every king after him. They've enslaved a race from the arctic circle to the north, the Enyos, to do a lot of the work. Being down in the mines isn't pretty business. It's dangerous. Nori, I'm sure you've noticed that mining is big business here in Parem too; but at least our workers do it willingly."

The conversation drifted as the men talked about politics that were unfamiliar to Mia. The discussion then turned toward the eastern country of Kai'Zi as they wondered whether anyone still lived in that massacred nation. That name of the country instantly rang a bell. Not being mistaken for a native of this enemy nation was the whole reason Mia had started dyeing her silver hair.

"Can you tell me more about Kai'Zi?" Mia wanted to know. "I've heard of it before, and I'm curious."

"It's a country in the northeast, where an arctic race lived," said Davern. "They gained a lot of wealth and political power, and they produced enough gold to rival Loriar. A couple hundred years ago, a tyrannical king of Loriar wanted to conquer the world, so he decided to start with Kai'Zi. Kai'Zi outsmarted Loriar that time and snuck into the country to assassinate the king and queen. Luck had it that the royal children were out in the country visiting a duke, and since the Kai'Zi assassin couldn't find them, their lives were spared and the royal line went on. Petty wars kept happening. And then about fourteen years ago, King Donorot the Fifth decided to gain control over Kai'Zi with a hostage. King Donorot's operatives sailed across the ocean and broke into the Kai'Zi palace, where King Dai'Ni and Queen Jai'Yaira lived. Must not have been an easy feat, since it's a cold, mountainous place and I'm sure there were plenty of guards. They kidnapped little Princess Jai'Zela, the heir to the throne. She was shipped to Loriar and held for a ransom. King Donorot said he would give the princess back only if Kai'Zi agreed to let Loriar take control of their gold mines, and never fight Loriar again."

"How old was this princess?" Mia asked.

"About three to four years old."

"That's so young."

"Loriar folks can be pretty ruthless when they have a goal to meet. Kai'Zi was of course not happy, and they sent some of their soldiers over to Loriar to try to get the little girl back. They were unsuccessful; the Loriar royal family had palace guards who killed them before they found the princess. Then King Dai'Ni and Queen Jai'Yaira resorted to a nasty tactic. Because King Donorot would not give the child back, the Kai'Zi sent a plague across the ocean in jars disguised as gifts. As soon as those jars were opened and people breathed that poison in, it spread from one person to another like wildfire."

"That's the plague that turned people's insides to liquid? I've heard a bit about it."

"Yes. It made its victims bleed from every orifice. One of the most brutal things to happen in all the history of mankind. The west lost so many people before we managed to stop it —thank heavens for that rabbit's blood medicine from south Parem."

"It's so upsetting to hear about this plague," Mia said. "I can understand being angry that the little girl was kidnapped, but I don't think it was worth all those people dying such a horrible death. What happened to the Loriar royals and the kidnapped princess?"

"They all caught the plague and died from it."

"I'm confused. So the Kai'Zi sent this plague here when the heir to their throne was here, and ended up killing her too?"

"The Kai'Zi probably figured that Queen Jai'Yaira was young and healthy, so she could produce another heir. That is the best explanation I can think of."

"The thought of forgetting about a dead child... a child that you killed... and having another to replace it... I just can't imagine," Mia gasped.

"The Kai'Zi were a sort of people who'd cut off their own leg to spite the enemy. They had a cold and ruthless mindset, like the scorpions of this desert, which will sting themselves to death if they're cornered. The Kai'Zi race had witch blood, and there is a theory that they were not fully human. I cannot verify that one, though."

"I heard that the Loriar royal family's bodies were never found," Rodrik chimed in. "Princess Jai'Zela wasn't found either. How can we be sure they're dead? What if they were hidden somewhere instead?"

"Oh, Rodrik, you and your silly conspiracy theories. Of course their bodies were found."

"It's not just a conspiracy theory. There are some searchers looking for those people to this day."

"But why? The searches will turn up nothing. They're

dead and they were immediately cremated to keep the disease from spreading. If they'd survived, King Donorot would still be sitting on the throne today. As for Princess Jai'Zela, they'd probably behead her and make a huge public event out of it. But that never happened, and they had to find some obscure duke to take the king's place. On with the story of the war. The whole west recruited massive armies. With some new and refined cannonballs and gunpowder, and some cutting-edge mechanical soldiers we designed right here at the university, the armies caught Kai'Zi by surprise and massacred the country. A lot of western soldiers were lost. The Kai'Zi were a hard race to defeat. With their witch blood, they could cast a few spells and control others' thoughts to some degree. But us Parem people are born resistant to mind witchery. And, of course, so were the mechanical soldiers, which had no minds for the Kai'Zi to get hold of. Those really helped the west to win the war. There's hardly a Kai'Zi person left standing today that I know of."

"So much history that I missed growing up on that island," Mia mused.

"From the looks of you, you were awfully young when all of that happened. And in a way, you were fortunate to be on that island. Because of the plague."

"True. My family never had it... I never even heard of it until I reached Dakoris."

"Not everyone was so lucky. I lost my mother to the plague. It was terrible."

"I'm really sorry to hear about that. I'm meeting so many people who have lost someone."

"Those mechanical soldiers really were something, I hear," Rodrik added.

"How did they work?" Mia wanted to know.

"I don't fully understand how they operated, since the royalty of Parem has worked hard to keep it a secret," Rodrik explained. "Even Davern doesn't know the whole story. But it had to do with gears."

"Very sophisticated gears," Davern added. "I wish I knew

what spurred them into motion, but those who know are tight-lipped about it to this day. The scientists and inventors at the university stayed up night after night in a hidden room underground. If you want, you can pass by the school, which is just down the street, and look at a replica of a mechanical soldier in the front garden."

"Does it have gears inside?" Mia's eyes sparkled with curiosity.

"No, it's just an empty shell. All of the working ones were retired after the war, and they're hidden away in some undisclosed location. I suppose the king and queen don't want commoners getting ideas, though a few of the scientists are working on creating a horseless carriage with those gears. Something that could travel farther and faster than any beast."

Mia sighed. "I'd love to take one of those things apart and get a good look inside. Gears... it's just so fascinating."

"A natural scientist." Davern smiled. "Maybe you should attend the university. I can tell you have the brain and the desire to learn that defines my best students. And you're in the right place, since women are allowed to study at the universities in Parem. But in Loriar, forget it."

"That sounds like a wonderful idea. I will definitely consider it when I return from Loriar."

"Before you go much further, you might want to consider paying a visit to Maraya, our local seer," Rodrik suggested. "She can give you some good insight on your journey."

"You know I'm skeptical of Maraya," Davern chided. "A woman who isn't of the witch race, but claims she can see into the future?"

"I can't think of a single time she's been wrong. Her house takes some work to get into. She lives on top of the stalk of sandstone that's by the cliff just north of town. So it'll be a bit of a hike and climb. But definitely worth your while."

"Thanks," said Mia. "I'll think about paying her a visit."

"It was nice speaking with you," Davern said, yawning. "But, night owls as we are, we'd best be turning in. Best of luck on your journey."

The two men left. Looking for something to occupy herself until she could check into an inn at sunrise, Mia left the tavern and rode in the direction of the university. It was a sprawling complex, its boxy sandstone structures bigger than most of the houses in the pale red city. It didn't take Mia long to find the replica of the mechanical soldier. With amazement, she dismounted her horse and circled around the copper and iron man-shaped thing, a few heads taller than she was and gripping a strange sticklike weapon in one of its artificial jointed hands. She studied the weapon and guessed that it operated with gunpowder. The mechanical soldier had no face, just a smooth, unsettling, cold surface on its oval head. She tapped on its sides, listening to the hollow ringing inside.

After checking in at the inn, Mia went to sleep underneath an open carved window with a thin white curtain fluttering in the breeze. She woke in the afternoon, while the sun was still out, and decided to go looking for the woman that Davern and Rodrik had mentioned. After asking for directions from a few passers-by, she located Maraya's home at a remote corner of the northern cliff. The horses could not possibly climb up there, so she hitched them to a tree down below and found some carved handholds in the rock face for her to ascend. Getting to the little house that was carved into the top also required some agility. As Mia walked across a narrow ridge of rock, she had to keep from looking down, or else her stomach did flip-flops.

Maraya's little house had no door, just a thin sheet strung in the doorway.

"Hello?" Mia called. "Anybody home?"

"Come in," said an old woman's wavering voice.

Mia pushed the sheet aside on the string and was hit with the sweet smell of incense. A short, squat woman sat cross-legged behind a round sandstone table. Her frizzy white hair, so long it might never have been cut, freely cascaded over her shoulders and her zigzagged robe. Mia's eyes were drawn to her huge pendant with a gleaming polished purple stone. Candles were lit on each edge of the table.

"Are you Maraya?" Mia asked.

"Yes, my dear. What is it you seek?"

"I'm on a trip to Beriniat, Loriar, to collect an inheritance to bring back to Dakoris," Mia explained.

"So you've come from Dakoris, eh?"

"Yes. It has been a rough journey. I was traveling with a married couple. The man was killed by an ahra and the woman died from a disease we caught. I got sick as well, but a healer nursed me back to health. I still feel a bit weak. But I'm getting better."

"The fact that you are continuing this journey alone speaks to an incredible strength and willpower."

"I don't really have anywhere else to go."

"What brought you to my home?"

"Last night, I spoke with a couple of gentlemen at the tavern, and they encouraged me to come visit you. They said that you could give me advice and see into the future."

"Well, then. Sit down, dear."

Mia knelt down on the floor, across the low table from the old woman. Maraya took something bundled with silky cloth and then unwrapped a cluster of small, angular crystals ranging in color from clear to pink to snow white. She smoothed the silk over the table and cupped her hands around the crystals, gently shaking them. She released them on top of the bluish silk. Mia wasn't sure what Maraya was doing as she leaned over the crystals and mumbled chants in a foreign, musical-sounding language. And then the woman's wrinkle-surrounded eyes snapped back up to Mia.

"This is one of the most powerful readings I've ever seen. You must learn who you truly are," Maraya announced. "To do so, you must face incredible dangers. Close brushes with your own death. Only then will you become more alive and aware."

"I've already had more brushes with death than I care to have," Mia grumbled.

"You are strong. You must be stronger still to continue on

the path to your destiny. In order to find your true destiny, you must venture first into the gaping maw of the monster itself. There will be great danger."

"The monster? You mean, literally, there's a monster?"

"Greater than just one creature. But only when you walk into the great fanged mouth, only when the sun begins to set, will the truth be revealed."

"What is the truth?"

Maraya chuckled. "That's for you to find out. Even the crystals cannot tell me how it will end for you. And only you are truly in control of your future."

"Do you think I'm doing the right thing by going to Beriniat by myself?"

"Look within your heart. Do you think it's the right thing to do? You have come this far, right? Keep going, and be prepared to receive your ultimate destiny." Maraya glanced back down at the sparkling crystals. "Oh, and know that true friendship lies ahead, too. Not just hardship. But should you remain here, you shall not find such friendship. You must go as soon as possible. Reach for the stars."

"Thank you, Maraya." Mia got up, dusted off her dress, and prepared to leave.

"Oh, one other thing," Maraya spoke up, clasping her withered fist around her large smooth pendant. "You do have a witch's wand in your possession, do you not?"

"Uh, yes. I don't think I showed it to you, did I? How do you know?"

Maraya smiled. "I have my ways of knowing things. Do not lose it, whatever you do. It may well come in handy. I wish you the best of luck in reaching your destiny. Be well."

Mia left the incense-filled hut, closing the sheet behind her, and picked her way back across the precarious pillars and path of sandstone and dirt. She wasn't sure whether the visit to that woman was just a waste of her time, and could not make sense of half the things she'd said. But the sun was getting lower in the sky and Mia figured it was time to go anyway. Well-prepared with food stores and full canteens, she unhitched the two horses and headed north.

Mia took a large highway as there were no faint trails marked on the map for this part of the world—though one began further north. The color of the desert changed from red to almost white. It was a low-traffic day, with hardly anyone else on the stretch of beaten-down road that led into the thicket of spindly, thorny trees bordering the wide Loris River. Mia reached a border outpost staffed with two armored men sitting in the shade of wooden huts, marking the entrance to Loriar. From the sides of the border outpost, vicious-looking fences made of thorny bramble stretched on into the sandy desert. These fences extended as far as the eye could see, dividing the two countries.

As she approached the twin huts, Mia could overhear the men's voices as they gossiped about the pair of night shift soldiers who would soon take their place. The conversation stopped at the sight of her.

One of the men, looking red, hot, and sweaty in his thick leather vest, raised a hand to halt Mia before she passed between the open huts. She gently tugged her horse's reins to stop him.

"Your name, please, ma'am,"

Mia faltered for a second as she remembered again the false name on the forged documents. "I'm Nori Tethlo."

The other man frowned, a distant look overtaking his dark brown eyes. "Ma'am, may I ask where you're from?"

"Dakoris."

"Are you traveling with a husband?"

"I'm not married."

"What is your business in Loriar?"

"Um... picking up an inheritance."

"An inheritance, huh? May I please see your documents?"

Feeling nervous and put on the spot, Mia fished around in one of her bags and produced the fake documents Tak had given her. The man took the parchment into his gloved hand and then handed it back to Mia. "Welcome to Loriar, Nori. Enjoy your stay in our fair country."

Loriar

Not long after Mia crossed through the border station and rode across the sturdy wooden bridge over the Loris River, the sun set. Once again, the desert looked stunning in the light from the moon, ring, and stars that painted the sand silver-white. As she trotted completely alone along the main highway, more and more unusual cacti began to pop up at the sides of the road, larger, with protrusions like arms and legs.

Just before the sun rose, Mia happened upon a village. Its architecture was nothing like the distinctive jungle ziggurats or sandstone dwellings she had become accustomed to in Parem. The simple, unimaginative frame houses were made from sun-bleached wood and had thatched roofs. When the sun came up, the local inn opened, and Mia rented a room, the most expensive room she had ever stayed in. Since she did not have Loriar coins, they charged her more.

Before bedding down, Mia ate breakfast in the dim, candle-lit dining area. The few other travelers wore drab gray and blue clothing, the women in dresses with puffy long sleeves and floor-length skirts that looked too hot and smothering for the weather. Their dark hair was scraped back in severe, tightly braided buns. Unlike the chatty and social people of Parem, these travelers did not speak and barely made eye contact with anyone else as they ate.

As Mia climbed the creaky stairs up to her room, a glob of tobacco-stained saliva landed on the front of her dress. Shocked, she looked up at the thin, older, hard-eyed man who'd spat on her. This had happened once before in Dakoris, likely because of her silver hair. But now, her hair was coated in dye, and she couldn't understand why this stranger sneered at her with such contempt in his eyes before he turned and walked away.

Mia already didn't like Loriar, and she was barely past the border. The professor was right in his criticisms. Maybe the inheritance wasn't worth a long trip though this place full of cold people. Maybe it was time to just give it up and turn around. And stick to the main highways—traveling alone, she could not go back through the ahra-infested jungle without certain death.

It was difficult for Mia to sleep underneath the thin, ratty quilt on the bed. Large jars of water kept the indoors cool enough, in contrast to the desert heat outside, but her naps were spotty at best. She awoke with a start at midday when voices came up from the main desk just below her room.

"Why, yes, a Nori Tethlo checked in not long after the break of dawn," the man working the desk said. "Why do you ask?"

"Why we ask is not your concern." Mia recognized this voice. It was one of the soldiers who'd been manning the border station she had passed through the previous evening. "In what room is she staying?"

"Just a second, I'll need to glance at the records."

Mia sprang out of bed, her heart pounding. She instinctively knew that she had to get out of here and fast, though she wasn't sure what those men would do to her if they did find her. She did not intend to wait around and find out. Gathering her things as fast as she could and throwing them into her sack, Mia ran to the window and looked down. Risking injury, she decided she had little choice but to jump. Mia dragged the skinny yet heavy down-filled mattress from the bed and pushed it out the window. It flopped down onto the hard, sandy ground below, raising a puff of dust. Mia then tossed out the bedding for extra padding. Closing her eyes, Mia said a silent prayer. Just as the door to the bedroom started to creak open, she let herself free-fall.

The painful, slamming impact nearly knocked Mia's breath out, though the mattress cushioned her from the sand beneath. She stood up, brushed herself off, and ran down the alleyway. As she turned the corner, a man shouted behind her. "Nori! Nori!"

Mia found her horses in the stable behind the inn and unhooked them as fast as she could, hands shaking on the ropes. She tied her bag to the front horse, mounted him, and firmly squeezed his midsection. The horse burst out running from the stable, with the pack horse thundering close behind. Mia's raven hair streamed behind her as she clung to the reins for dear life, guiding the horses through the packed-down dirt village streets, surprising the few people out and walking in the heat.

Fearing that it wasn't safe to stay on the main highway, as there was no doubt now that she was being closely followed, Mia took the risk of getting lost and veered into territory unmarked on her map. The horses ran across a dry riverbed edging the village, through a thicket of trees and cacti that hid them all for a while, and into the expanse of desert beyond.

With the ring to the south, Mia hoped to keep track of her position without a trail to follow, at least for now. She guessed that by the position of the boiling sun, currently she was going east, vaguely in the direction of the capital city—but right now, safety and finding a place to hide were the most important goals. Mia periodically glanced over her shoulder, and as the village faded into a tiny dot on the white sand, she breathed a sigh of relief to see no one behind her. She had gotten away just barely in the nick of time.

After a while of frantic running, Mia grew concerned that the horses' hooves left behind shallow impressions in the sand. However, this land was grassier than the red desert of Parem further down south. With any luck, the large patches of pale green grass, dotted with a few flowers, would help to conceal the tracks. The landscape grew hillier and hillier as Mia passed many a tall cactus, from which pale red rose-like flowers grew. She had to stop and dismount for a while when her horse brushed his shoulder against a cactus arm and whinnied in pain. Stroking the horse to keep him calm, she pulled out the spines and then dabbed a small amount of herbal tincture from Mendy's pack onto the bleeding puncture wounds. After a rushed food and water break, Mia and her two horses carried on again at a fast pace.

When she camped out that evening, the exhausted Mia found a rock outcropping with a hollow below. This one even had a water spring, reflecting its ever-moving waves on the arch of rock that concealed it. Mia and the horses happily drank, and she bathed away the sweat that had streamed down her body, joyfully refreshed afterward. Mia decided not to risk attracting attention with a campfire tonight. Succumbing to exhaustion, she fell asleep in the shade on a soft patch of grass.

Mia woke in the morning. Though she would have preferred to keep moving at night, she didn't want to waste time, especially when she looked back to the southeast and grew anxious at the faint clouds of dirt being kicked up in the distance. Mia filled her canteen as fast as she could, packed up, and made the horses break out into a full run again.

By the late afternoon, Mia could tell that the horses were nearing exhaustion, their energy depleted by the pitiless sun bearing down upon all of them. Not wanting to harm the horses, Mia had no choice but to stop for the day. She hopped down from her horse and led him by the reins to the nearest shade underneath a few blooming trees, the only large vegetation in sight other than the cacti that were now thinning out in number. She sat down and gave the horses bowls of water. On the northeastern horizon, above the waving mirage created by the heat, teal mountains had appeared. Gray clouds also dotted the sky, but none were big enough to produce rain.

"Hey, fellows," Mia said to the horses, "look over there. I bet there are some lush forests in those mountains. Nice and shady and cool. If we keep going, we'll be there in no time."

The horses gazed wearily back at her, sagging their large heads.

Mia opened one of the packs and took out the witch's wand. It had been on her mind ever since Maraya, the seer back in Parem, urged her to hang on to it. Mia sat on a rock and turned the wooden rod over and over in her hands, studying the way the crystal at the top glittered in the sun. The wand did not look particularly special or magical, just a gem strapped to a stick.

Mia looked up and saw it again—the puffs of sand rising up in the distance, back the way she had come. Today, she and the horses had traversed long stretches of sand, meaning she'd left behind obvious tracks for that man from the border station and whoever else was looking for Mia to follow.

"Oh no," Mia sighed out loud to the horses. "I think those strange men may be after me again. I just wish I knew why they're so interested in me, even though I told them that false name. I wish I knew whatever it is that people aren't telling me. Come on, fellows. We've got to use the last of our strength. Let's go."

When she tugged at each horse's reins, they stubbornly whinnied and lowered their heads in defiance. She sensed that if she pushed them any harder, they could run themselves to death.

Mia muttered in her anxiety and fear. The dust clouds off to the west looked slightly bigger. So did the clouds up above, though big bands of blue sky still showed between them.

Mia sighed, putting her head in her hands, wishing she could figure out a good way to cover her tracks and not kick up a big cloud of dust. She felt out of options, not sure what else to do.

Defeated, Mia sat on a rock for a while, hands over her eyes, pressing the wand to her cheek. If she came close to getting caught, she could assume her wolf form as a last resort. But if the horses saw her in the body of a predator, they would bolt away in terror. And she needed them.

When Mia parted her fingers and peeked through them, the sky was suddenly much darker. Propelled by brisk winds, storm clouds merged together, burgeoning with rain. One cloud off in the distance was already raining, the sheets of moisture drying up before they hit the ground. And the delicious earthy smell of impending rain was beginning to fill the air.

"Yes!" Mia said aloud. "If it rains—really rains—that will be excellent! It'll wash away the tracks, and dampen the dust!"

As if on cue, thunder rumbled and lightning flashed white across the wide-open landscape. The rain started to come down —first a few fat droplets cold and trickling down Mia's cheeks, and then heavier and heavier, pouring in sheets as lightning bolts continued to crackle. It had been a long time since chilly rain slammed down upon her, and it weighed down her short-sleeved cloak. The plummeting temperature felt refreshing and divine, like plunging into the cool spring under the rock the day before.

The horses appreciated the rain, too, as it matted down their coats. After resting for a short while, they all felt well enough to continue on. Mia slung herself onto the wet saddle, and this time she allowed the horses to walk at an easy pace. This gray world of pouring rain brought Mia to a level of ecstasy she hadn't experienced in a long time. Since the deaths of her traveling companions, she had not felt much at all except for fear and the will to survive.

Unfortunately, the clouds covered the sun, ring, and mountains to the northwest, making it impossible to be certain in what direction Mia was going. She stayed in a straight line and hoped that she was at least on the right track. When she glanced behind her, nothing indicated she was being followed, though in the thick sheets of rain she couldn't see quite as far except in the moments when lightning made the land glow. During those split seconds, Mia could never be sure if there were any figures far off.

The rain continued to pour well into the night. By then, Mia was cold, her clothes soaked through and through, but it still didn't bother her. A complication was the mud. To avoid the horses' legs getting sucked in, Mia began keeping to the rockier areas. Amid the muddy dirt, channels of running water flooded across Mia's path from time to time, glinting in the flashes of lightning.

The rain finally let up, and the silvery clouds parted. After the gloom, the stars sparkled more brilliantly than ever. Mia found a camp site on relatively high ground, unlikely to flood, and decided to set up her tent. Mia longed to have a fire to warm up and dry off, but finding any dry kindling was unlikely, and she still did not want to make herself easy to spot. She went to sleep soaking wet and shivering, with clumpy damp hair clinging to her face.

When Mia woke in the morning, she wasted no time in continuing on. The sun was back out today, with not a cloud in the blue sky. Evidence of yesterday's heavy rainstorm still lay in the dark, muddy ground. The horses' tracks from the journey's previous leg were long gone and washed away, and Mia no longer kicked up a cloud of dust, but now the soaked earth carried new, deep impressions of their hooves. Avoiding the mud was not always possible as Mia progressed on toward the mountains. The tall cacti with the arms and legs vanished, now replaced with small dry evergreen-smelling bushes and a few trees. The buildings of a village rose up on the far northern horizon, but Mia decided not to risk being around other people right now. Hopefully the heavy rainstorm had made those men lose track of her or give up the search altogether.

Late in the afternoon, Mia traveled through a patch of especially difficult mud. The horses struggled, their legs getting drawn into the muck. And then came a snapping noise and a pained cry behind her. Mia stopped and climbed down from the saddle, finding her pack horse trapped in mud against a rock, writhing frantically. When he finally dug his way out, the limpness and unnatural angle in his front leg was not a good sign. Unable to walk on the broken leg, he fell over onto his side, moaning.

"No!" Mia screamed. Danli had taught her about the poor prognosis when a horse broke its leg. And on a long journey like this with no opportunity for rest in sight, the outlook was especially grave. Danli would have recommended putting this horse out of his misery. She had kept a farrier's axe in case this situation happened, to deliver a sharp final blow to the wounded horse's head with its spiked back end. Mia had no such axe.

"Oh no," Mia shouted again, kneeling in the wet mud beside the moaning horse. She stroked his cheek and mane, wanting to cry at the very thought of the next step. She'd hunted animals for food, but this horse was part of the only family she had left. She couldn't kill him. She just couldn't.

Yet she couldn't leave him here to die slowly in the sun either.

"I'm sorry," Mia whispered to the pack horse, stroking him again and leaning down to kiss him on the head. His eye darted around in fright. She went to the packs on the other horse and fished out Tak's knife. As she stood over the downed horse, knife at the ready, she said a prayer for a painless passage into the arms of the sheep-goddess in the afterlife, and then faltered.

Sobbing, Mia sliced across the horse's throat, the hardest thing she'd ever done. Guilt tortured her as he whinnied and struggled, blood pouring into the sand. After the fight left his body and his eyes went glassy, Mia held the pack horse's still-warm body and cried and wailed into his mane. She removed his packs and put what she could on the other horse, sacrificing some food that had spoiled, one of the blankets, and the fake documentation, which she tore up until it was unrecognizable. People were looking for her under the name Nori now, so it would no longer do her any good.

Mia went on, brokenhearted and numb she rode into the foothills of the mountains late the following night. She passed a strange ring of stones with swirled manmade carvings in their sunbaked faces. Two figures, one masculine and virile, one rounded and female.

∞∞∞

Not long after Mia worked her way up into the mountains, the shrubby dry vegetation turned into tall, lofty pine trees.

They were similar to the ones she remembered in Dakoris, but larger, more majestic, with redder trunks that gave off a sweet scent. The terrain was quite rocky, with some tenacious pine trees growing right out of cliff tops or cracks in the rocks. Mia was forced onto a circuitous path because of the cliffs, rocky obstacles, and mountains too steep to climb. The air, though still as dry as the desert, was considerably cooler up here. Mia found a creek trickling with icy snow runoff, and a small spring to bathe in. The ice-cold water shocked her whole body.

She also stumbled across a few ruins of ancient buildings, some more stones with carvings of the god and goddess whose worship was now forbidden, and an abundance of animals to hunt with the crossbow. At night, Mia built fires to cook the small critters she caught and warm up by the coals. Though the surrounding trees helped Mia feel a little bit more closed in, concealed from view, and safe, they also teemed with darkness and danger, especially at night. She couldn't see what was ahead or what was behind, even in broad daylight. And if there were any monsters, Mia had no one to warn her about them, having not spoken to any human beings in a while.

One day, faint shouts echoed from the distance. Slowly, she followed the direction of the sounds, coming upon the first sign of current human activity since escaping the desert. A wooden fence surrounded a mine shaft dug into a pine-needle-dusted hill. Pale, sickly-looking men and women, wearing little more than tattered loincloths, pulled carts out of the mine. The carts were heaping with mounds of dirt, glinting with flecks of gold. The workers' yellowish hair, dirty and unwashed, clung to their large heads. More of these zombie-like people hunched over a large wooden contraption running with water, shaking gold loose from clots of dirt with sieves.

A young woman lingering close to the fence noticed Mia on the other side. She turned, stunned like an animal caught in a trap, her pale, almost colorless eyes huge like an owl's. Her almost-naked body was a heartbreaking bag of bones, her bare breasts little more than empty sacks hanging from arching ribs.

"You... you shouldn't be here," the woman whispered weakly.

"Why not?"

The woman turned and walked away.

Too curious about what was going on to simply leave, Mia hung around deep in the trees, watching from afar. She made herself a camp as evening descended, creeping around behind trees to observe the activity at the mine.

At nightfall, a dark-haired man showed up on horseback, cracking a whip and ordering the emaciated people into a large, cage-like pen near the mine. Once they had all been crammed inside, the man gave them a few bowls of mushy food like a pack of dogs, and then slammed a great metal door shut, clicking a padlock closed to secure it.

The sight of enslaved human beings, wasting away and living in misery, angered and sickened Mia. As soon as the man rode away on his well-groomed black horse, Mia crept down the hill toward the massive cage. At the sound of her approach, the slaves shrunk back in fright.

"Hello," Mia called to them. "Don't worry, I'm not going to hurt you. How long have you been stuck here?"

A man stuttered, his mouth almost completely toothless. "Ah... ah... for most of us, we've been here all our lives, miss."

"You don't like living like this, do you?"

A woman spoke up, her pale hair clinging to her gaunt face, her lower lip trembling. "We've no choice. We were born Enyos."

"Enyos?"

"That's our race. They... they keep us as slaves. Just the way it is..." She faltered.

Mia glanced at the ground near her feet, finding a large rock. Picking it up, she swung it hard at the lock on the cage door. After three hard blows, the lock, made from iron, refused to break apart. Mia decided to try something else, just in case it might work, though she doubted it would. On impulse, she pulled the witch's wand from the bag she wore at her belt and pressed the crystal to the lock.

"If you really work," she whispered, "open this lock."

Ever so slightly, energy vibrated through the wand. With a resonant click, the lock released. Mia, unable to believe her eyes, gasped in wonderment and pulled it off the door, swinging it wide open.

"You all are free to go," she called to the slaves. "This is your chance to escape."

"But... but..." the woman muttered. "We can't just... run."

"Yes, you can. Run. Now. And don't look back."

Finally, it sank in for the Enyo slaves that all of them were being liberated. Cautiously, some of them stepped outside of the cage, and then bolted into the trees and vanished. They left behind the nauseating stink of the urine and feces they had probably been forced to marinate in for years.

The ones who remained worked themselves up into an excited frenzy. "More food," they cried. "We get more food."

Unable to convince the stragglers to leave, Mia packed up her camp and rode further east, making sure to put a generous distance between herself and the mine until she set up another camp in the middle of the night.

As Mia woke up late in the morning and cooked breakfast over the smoldering coals of her campfire, something rustled in the trees behind her. A haunted face peeked out between the tall red trunks.

"Hello?" Mia called.

A barefoot young teenager came into view, her body streaked with dirt. She wore only a filthy wrap around her rib-ridged waist. Long pale golden hair fell down her back, matted into dreadlocks that reminded Mia of her father.

"Do you have any food you can spare?" she whispered.

Mia gave her a few small strips of jerky. She gobbled them ravenously, licking her fingers.

"Have you lived in that wretched pen your whole life?" Mia wanted to know.

"Yes. I was born inside it."

"Isn't it awfully dirty in there?" Mia's stomach turned at the thought of women giving birth on the ground in the smelly pen. Danli had provided private stables lined with fresh clean straw when her animals had babies. Were these slaves given even that luxury?

"It's just the way it is."

"Wouldn't it get cold in that pen? What about winters?"

"Of course it gets cold." She held up a hand, with the pinky and ring finger just stumps. "They give us blankets and furs. We huddle together."

"I didn't notice children in the pen. Were there any?"

"Just a few. There are less children every year. Mr. Totlok tries to make babies with some of the girls. He tried with me once."

"Mr. Totlok?"

"The man who owns the mine."

"Do you know where he is right now?"

"No, I don't. There's no doubt he is looking for us."

"I'm glad you're away from that terrible man. Starving people, keeping them in a dirty cage, taking advantage of the women... what kind of a man is this?"

The girls' eyes grew cloudy and troubled. "Mr. Totlok really isn't such a terrible man. It's just what we miners have to do."

"They have to make people live in deplorable conditions?"

"It gets things done. We dig up gold for our masters. Everyone has to. I... I have to help Mr. Totlok. I can't just run off." She pushed her weakened body up off the rock where she sat.

"Where are you going?" Mia wanted to know. "Don't tell me you feel sorry for that man!"

"Where else am I going to go?" the young woman wailed.

"Look at you. I can see your ribs and hipbones. You're starving."

"But I can't find food out here. Mr. Totlok will feed me."

"It's not enough, obviously. I have food in my packs and I know how to hunt and prepare meat. I know how to find fruits and berries that are good to eat. The wilderness will feed you better than Mr. Totlok did."

There was a rustle in the trees, and out came another young Enyo woman. "Come on, come on!" she cried. "We have to run! Mr. Totlok is after us!"

"But we might have to go back," the girl protested.

"No, no! Please come!"

Both of them dashed into the trees. Left behind by herself, Mia began to quickly pack her things, hoping to outrun this Mr. Totlok in case he was making his way in this direction. She hurriedly attached her packs to her horse and trotted away.

As the thick forest went past, the hoofbeats of another horse drew closer and closer. Mia squeezed her own mount with her legs, encouraging him to run as fast as he could.

The horse wailed. Mia was tossed from the saddle as he fell to the ground. She landed hard on her side, knocking the wind out of her. Gasping, Mia sat up, dirty and dazed. Her horse lay on his side as his outstretched legs twitched. A bolt from a crossbow stuck up from his shoulder. Blood trickled down.

Mia ran to her horse, falling to her knees and pulling slowly upward on the bolt to remove it. As she tugged, it seemed to dig deeper into the horse's flesh, making him screech in agony.

"Stop right there, wretched woman," a deep male voice ordered. Mia looked up at the slave master on his black horse, aiming his crossbow straight at her. "Yes, you've got the right idea. Don't make a move. Do you know much about Loriar arrows and bolts?"

Backing away and trembling, Mia slowly shook her head no.

"If you try to pull one out, it's futile. They have barbs in 'em that come out if there's resistance. Do you want to cooperate with me, or do you want to die?"

The olive-skinned man dismounted his horse and approached the anxious Mia, still aiming his crossbow at her. Mia wished that she had thought to arm herself with the dagger before taking off from her campsite. Instead, it was tucked away in a bag attached to her wounded horse.

"You're going to come with me," the man snarled. Up close, his dark brown eyes were cold, like polished stones. Eyes with no empathy behind them. "I overheard you. I know you're the one who robbed me of my Enyo helpers. Some of them took off. And now the rest of them are going mad. I don't need to be put through this kind of strain. My wife is due to bear my son any day!"

He gripped Mia by the arm with an iron fist and yanked her along, away from her groaning, dying horse. She tripped and fell and he nearly dislocated her arm pulling her up again.

As Mia came to her senses, she decided to fight back. She balled up her fist, swung it around, and punched him in the jaw as hard as she could.

Mr. Totlok bellowed. Instead of loosening his grip in his pain, he clenched his free hand and hit Mia back on the side of her head. Stars flickered across her vision as she was thrown to the ground.

Mia flung her fists and kicked, aiming for the most delicate areas even as her filthy dress hindered the movement of her legs. They rolled on the dirt and brawled as bolts spilled out of Mr. Totlok's quiver. Mia split Mr. Totlok's lip and he gave her a black eye as blood dribbled from his chin. And then a blow to her head rendered her unconscious. Everything went black.

Mia woke up, her head throbbing and her hairline crusted with a bit of dried blood. Her eyes blurred, and then focused on the bars of the slave pen as its foul smell wafted around her. Mia slowly sat up and found herself surrounded with bars, locked inside the pen by herself. Where had the remaining slaves gone? Without the dagger or wand or any of her other things, there was probably nothing Mia could do to get out of this pen. She was Mr. Totlok's slave now, and quite possibly his next kill.

She had to think, and think fast.

∞ ∞ ∞

Mr. Totlok angrily marched toward the slave pen, having earlier ordered the lingering slaves to leave and find the escapees. He carried ominous tools—a club and a dagger among them. A sharp-jawed trap dragged along the ground on a chain behind him. A lecherous grin crossed his face in anticipation.

It was evening, and the sun was going down, shining in rays between the pines. Mr. Totlok approached the smelly slave pen and twisted his key in the lock. In the shadows, something snarled viciously.

"Where did you go?" Mr. Totlok demanded to know. "You're going to pay, you whore! You're going to pay for what you did to me!"

Slamming the door behind him in his rage, he dragged his torture instruments into the pen. He peeked around, looking for the girl and seeing no sign of her in the shadows. And then something glinted, metallic silver. Inhuman eyes shone at him from a dark corner of the pen. Mr. Totlok froze, a chill going down his spine.

Something circled him, growling and baring white fangs. His jaw dropped as a silver wolf stared him straight in the eye.

"Damn it," Mr. Totlok muttered, his voice muted in fear. He threw the trap at the wolf. It snapped shut as the animal deftly darted back into the shadows.

Charging at the creature, Mr. Totlok frantically swung his club. The wolf dodged every blow, and then jumped up, lunging for his neck.

∞ ∞ ∞

Mia walked away from the pen, wiping the fresh, salty blood away from her mouth and scrubbing her hands with dirt. The gravity of taking a man's life weighed on her, even in this obvious act of self-defense.

It was too late for Mia's last standing horse. While she was locked away, Mr. Totlok had finished him off and then stolen

Mia's packs.

Tears filling her eyes, Mia ran in one direction, and then the other, in the darkness. All around, the trees chittered with squirrels and insects.

Shrouded in shadows was a tall, gloomy stone manor, not far from the gold mine. Mia ran toward it and pounded on the ivy-bordered door, hoping for help, though she wasn't sure how much anyone could help her at this point.

Someone unlatched the heavy door, and then it creaked open, revealing an interior lit with torches and a very pregnant woman with brown hair pulled back in a bun. Her belly pooched out in her pink nightgown. She held up a candle, lighting up Mia's face. Mia looked down, knowing that the shine in her eyes frightened some people.

"Who are you?" the woman asked. This was probably Mr. Totlok's wife, unaware she was now a widow. Mia had to make a conscious effort to push away the guilt over a child growing up fatherless.

"I'm, uh, lost, and both of my horses died. Someone robbed me."

"Do you need a warm bed and some food?"

"Yes, if you are able to help me. I'll continue on my journey after that."

The woman sputtered. "Well, I... I'll have to speak with my husband first. And he is not in right now."

"By any chance, are you Mrs. Totlok?"

"That's me."

"I'm very sorry, Mrs. Totlok." Mia kept her eyes down. "Your husband is no longer with us."

"Really, now?! What on earth?"

"I, erm, saw his death. It happened very quickly, in the slave pen. An animal of some sort attacked him."

"And you ran away?"

"Yes. I'm sorry."

"The thing probably would have gotten you, too, if you hadn't run. These woods are full of dangers." The woman's eyes gleamed with a burst of wetness, and she put a fist up to her mouth to hold back a moan. Quickly, Mrs. Totlok composed herself. "I suppose I've nothing left to lose if I let you stay here a night. Follow me."

As they walked down the dim hall, Mia noticed some bundles sitting on a wooden table off to the side. Her packs. "Mrs. Totlok? Those are my things."

"My husband came into the house very agitated this evening, carrying those sacks with him. He would not tell me what was going on."

"I hate to tell you this. He killed my horse and took my things."

"I am sorry he did that. He has been very angry for the past day or so. You may have your things back."

"Thank you."

They walked up a flight of creaking wooden stairs, Mrs. Totlok waddling and supporting her back with a hand. The woman led Mia to a bedroom with soft sheets, a bearskin rug before the fireplace, and velvet curtains on the window.

"This is very nice," Mia said. "The nicest room I've ever seen. Thank you."

"How long will you stay? Where are you going?"

"I shall probably just stay a day or two, unless you need help, since it appears that you're due any day."

"Don't worry about me. Really." Mrs. Totlok didn't seem nearly as distressed as Mia had expected over the loss of her husband. After that first shocked bout of misty eyes, she looked perfectly calm and composed. Maybe it would sink in later, the bad news of what Mia herself had done.

"If you say so, but I'm still not sure I want to leave you alone when your baby is this close to arriving," Mia said. "I'm on my way to Beriniat."

"That's where my family lives," Mrs. Totlok explained. "Now that I am a widow, I will need Father's help to get our affairs in order. While you're there, would you mind paying him a visit?"

"I don't see why not. How do I find your father?"

"His name is Rovett Tenor. He is a priest at the Temple of the God of All on the south side of the city. Please tell him I've been widowed, and then he'll know what to do from there."

"I'll do it as soon as I get there."

The God of All—that was the god Mia grew up hearing stories about on the island. Another piece of evidence fell into place to confirm that her family came from Loriar.

"If you need anything at all, ring this bell." Mrs. Totlok instructed, lifting a silver bell from a table and shaking it. A servant girl appeared at her side. This girl was an Enyo, but unlike the gaunt outdoor slaves Mia had freed, she was full-figured and wore a floor-length blue dress. Her skin looked clean, pale blond hair neatly groomed into a braided bun.

"If this young lady—I'm sorry, what's your name?" Mrs. Totlok asked.

"Uh... Ani." Since people had been chasing after Mia under the name of Nori, she came up with a new alias on the spot.

"If Ani needs anything, anything at all, please attend to her."

"Yes, ma'am. Mrs. Totlok, I have something I need to tell you." The servant leaned toward Mrs. Totlok and whispered into her ear. Mrs. Totlok furrowed her brow and slapped her forehead with her palm.

"Ani, is it true that you released my husband's mine slaves?"

Mia admitted the truth. "Yes, I did. Mrs. Totlok, they were starving. They looked sick. I'm sorry, but I couldn't stand it."

"Some of them would not leave," the house servant meekly brought up. "But then Mr. Totlok made them leave to search for the others. I'm not certain when they'll be back. Or if they'll come back."

Mrs. Totlok turned back towards Mia. "Ani, I don't know whether to be angry at you or whether... whether to congratulate you."

At that last part of the sentence, the house servant could

not conceal her expression of surprise.

"Congratulate me?" Mia asked, confused.

"I knew that he wasn't feeding them enough. He cut their rations to line his pockets with more money. They would die, one after the other. They could no longer fall pregnant. They began eating their own dead—isn't that sickening? My husband's business would fall apart if they all got too sick to work, if they all died. But the one time I decided to speak up about my concerns, well..." Mrs. Totlok trailed off, her lower lip beginning to tremble.

"What happened then?"

"I was... I was punished."

"Punished?"

"After he almost killed me, he stormed off and took out his rage on one of the house servants. She did not survive."

The servant standing next to Mrs. Totlok frowned and went pale.

"This all sounds like such a nightmare." Mia's guilt at killing Mr. Totlok started to slowly trickle away, even as the gravity of what she'd done sunk in.

"I suppose that you could say that particular nightmare is over. But now I am without a husband and don't know what to do. I hope Father gets here quickly."

"I'll go see him promptly when I get to the capital. But I'm sure it will take a while to get there."

"Let me ask you this, Ani. Where did you come from?"

"It's a long story. I came up from Dakoris. But my family is from Loriar."

"What part of Loriar are they from?"

"I don't know. My family is dead. They never told me."

After the two ladies left the room, Mia had trouble falling asleep. She waited for Mrs. Totlok or her house servant to change their minds and seek revenge with a dagger in her sleep, or even for Mrs. Totlok to accuse Mia of killing her husband. Even in her wolf form, in the wild body that craved raw flesh, killing a man had not been an emotionally easy feat. Even if it was a man who had beaten his wife, murdered a housekeeper, and starved his workers out of greed.

Mia got up at sunrise, earlier than usual, more well-rested than she had been in a very long time after a night in the softest and most comfortable she'd ever slept in. Hungry, Mia put on her dirty dress and walked down the hall, past the open door of the opulent master bedroom, lined with richly designed wood carvings and a marble fireplace.

Mrs. Totlok stood in front of a mirror beside the fireplace, shaking and combing her brown hair. The widowed woman was clad only in her undergarments.

Last night when Mia went to bed, Mrs. Totlok was nine months pregnant. But now, somehow, she had a flat, taut belly.

Lingering in the doorway and watching as Mrs. Totlok dragged a wooden comb through her hair, Mia listened for the cry of a newborn. She peeked quickly around the bedroom for bassinets, bloody sheets or rags, or bowls of water—any evidence of a birth overnight. There were no wailing babies, no swaddling blankets. And Mia had not heard anything last night, either. Though Mia was tired, she couldn't imagine sleeping through the screams of a woman in labor in the next room.

Until now, Mia had never seen an unclothed woman right after childbirth, but she doubted that a stomach could snap back to its former state that quickly. Wouldn't it look puffy or sag down after being stretched out that far?

Something was odd here. Too odd for Mia to be able to keep her mouth shut.

"Did you just have your baby?" Mia called out, unable to contain her surprise. Mrs. Totlok spun around, startled.

"Where's your baby?" Mia asked. "I didn't hear a thing last night. Perhaps you had a painless labor? Isn't it soon to be up and walking?"

"Oh, all right, I'll show you my baby," Mrs. Totlok sighed. She turned around and picked up a bundle that rested on a wooden chair. A sewn, stuffed cloth pad with a strap on the back.

"If you don't mind me asking," Mia said, "why were you

pretending to be an expectant mother?"

"Let me put my dress on, and then I'll explain," Mrs. Totlok pulled on her pink dress. Sewn specifically for the late stages of pregnancy, its empty front scrunched over her belly. Sagging her head, she looked toward her fireplace. "He wouldn't hit me, wouldn't even touch me, when I was with child. He didn't want to harm the baby in case it was the boy he'd hoped for all these years. I was tired of the beatings, wondering when he'd kill me. Starting to feel like it was only a matter of time. I have not fallen pregnant for the past couple of years, but I came up with this idea and sewed these pads late at night while he slept. It may sound nutty. But the more desperate you get, the stranger your ideas get."

"Did you think about running away from him?"

"I don't think I could have gotten far. He would've had people looking for me. He is—was—a very important man, and he had a lot of connections. I was too frightened."

"If you don't mind me asking, how were you going to explain it when you were due to give birth?"

"I've already paid off a midwife to tell him when the time came that the baby was stillborn. And I figured that I would wait a while, and then start putting the pads under my dresses again."

"And then you'd say you had another stillbirth?"

"Something like that, yes."

"Mrs. Totlok, do you have actual children?"

Mrs. Totlok's eyes moistened. "The babies. I had three of them. And I... I never saw them again. I did not even have the chance to nurse them. The poor dears."

"What happened?"

"They were all girls." Mrs. Totlok choked back a raw, heavy, barking sob. "And... well... my husband wanted a son, of course. I could not give him a son. Every time the midwife came out and told him it was a girl, he went berserk, kicking and smashing things. And then he would demand to see the baby. After that, I'd never see them again."

"Oh, no."

"When I asked him what happened to our daughters, he always had excuses, saying they were kidnapped, or they got fever, or they suffocated in their cradles. And then I found out from the servants that he... got rid of them. Because they weren't sons." Tears streamed down Mrs. Totlok's face.

"I... I can't imagine. I'm so sorry." Mia put an arm around the crying woman. "I can't imagine how horrible that must have been! Why would he do such a thing?"

"You say your family's from Loriar. But you didn't grow up here."

"No. I didn't."

"That's just the way it is here. I was very fortunate that my father kept me even if he was disappointed. My girls weren't so lucky."

"Again, I'm so sorry. About everything that's happened."

"I suppose I'm numb right now. I don't feel much of anything. I don't believe I'll be needing this 'baby' anymore." Ruefully, Mrs. Totlok tossed the fat cushion she had worn underneath her dress into the fire. The cloth curled away as the straw inside it began to crackle and sizzle.

For the next three days, Mia remained with Mrs. Totlok and her servant. The widow swung back and forth between different emotions. Sometimes she felt the last remnants of confused longing for her savage late husband, the fear that she could not manage on her own, and a bit of grief. Though Mrs. Totlok did not deny that he had been a terrible man, she had fallen in love with him at one time, and it was hard to let go of what little bit of that she had left. And what was she going to do now, with the slaves freed from the mine that was her source of income?

Wanting Mrs. Totlok and her servant to be prepared in case they ran out of food while they waited to hear back from the widow's father, Mia taught them some survival tips. She showed them how to walk softly and slowly through the woods without breaking so much as a single twig. She had them practice with arrows to hunt game and demonstrated the art of creating traps. Mia watched as the two women tried their new skills on squirrels, gutting them and hanging tiny strands of their flesh on twigs over a fire. Mia did not know how to identify all of the berries and plants of Loriar, but she pointed out the same thing she had mentioned to Tak and Mendy: if the animals left a plant untouched, there was probably a reason.

After growing up in a hut in the woods, the Enyo house servant was a wellspring of wilderness knowledge. Toward the end of Mia's stay at the home, both Mia and Mrs. Totlok learned a lot about the local vegetation from her.

∞∞∞

Mia still had business to attend to in Beriniat. Though she felt bad leaving, Mia finally decided to go on her way, wishing her hosts well, and promising to locate Mrs. Totlok's father once she reached the eastern city of Beriniat.

Mrs. Totlok only had one horse, the one belonging to her late husband, and wanted to keep it in case she needed to travel. Mia departed on foot, leaving some of her things behind for her hostess to use. Mia wore her most essential possessions, as well as the dagger and wand, in a leather sack strapped to her back. The pack hung heavily as she walked.

With only Mia's feet to carry her, this part of the journey became frustratingly slow. The daylight lasted for a long time each day, but it got chilly in the mornings and evenings and downright cold at night.

One evening, Mia came across an old fur trapper living in a ramshackle log cabin by an icy stream. His cabin reeked from the urine-based solutions he used to tan hides. Rabbit, skunk, and ermine skins dangled from the wooden overhang of his front porch as he busied himself tanning a stretched hide with carved bone tools.

Mia was hungry for food and also for human contact. She dreamed of how nice it would be if someone invited her in and offered her space in front of a roaring fireplace, a hot meal, and nice, plush bed to sleep on underneath a thick blanket. When Mia approached the grizzled old man to say hello, he leered at her from his porch, looking her up and down.

"What's a girl doing on her own in these woods?" he asked. "You look so tired. Like you need a good bed to rest in."

Only then did Mia realize just how exhausted she was. A bone-deep kind of tired. "Do you have a spare bed?"

"I could make a cozy sleeping spot in front of the hearth. I've also got good rabbit stew over the fire."

"Thank you so much! Thank you, thank you!"

"You don't need to fall over yourself thankin' me. Come in. Have some stew!"

After Mia went into the cabin and helped herself to bland, oily stew—which she conceded was better than what she'd had over the past few days—the man did not say much to her. He stayed out on his porch, working and scraping, until evening. He came in late to roast some strips of rabbit meat over the fire, feeding Mia a piece. They shared bitter, home-brewed beer.

The bed that the old trapper made for Mia was simple, one fur pelt on his wood floor, a sack stuffed with cloth for a pillow, and another pelt as a blanket. The animal fur prickled Mia as she tried to get comfortable. The exhaustion took over and she drifted off.

Mia was awakened in the middle of the night with a hand on her hip, the man curled behind her. "Hey, pretty girl," a hot raspy whisper came into her ear. "Been a long, long time since I've seen a young thing such as yourself. Let's get that dress off."

"No!" Mia shouted, sitting up.

"How dare you tease me?" The man's expression turned cruel. "A young beauty waltzes right into my house, and then denies me?!"

Mia grabbed her belt and her sack and sped for the door. The man chased her, again grabbing at her dress. She kicked him, leg shooting out backwards. He fell to the floor with a grunt as she fastened on her shoes.

Mia made haste off into the trees, getting as far away from that cabin as she possibly could. She set up a solitary camp that night, not building a fire. Remembering the lurid look on the trapper's face, a little too much like the hunger in her brother Deto's eyes, Mia felt a little too uneasy to get much sleep that night. She tossed and turned in the chill of the night.

Days later, Mia's feet got blisters from all the walking, and she had to set up a camp and take a short hiatus. She pressed herbal poultices to her feet to avoid infection and pain, and rested in her tent whenever possible. She set up a campfire and roasted meat on a pyramid of sticks and cooked soup to tide herself over. Once her feet healed, she started again.

After days of trudging alone through the woods, crossing steep rocky ravines and mountainsides, Mia came upon a beautiful spring, large and shimmering. Encrusted in sweat after the relentless walking, she was desperate for a bath. After refilling her canteen with the pristine water, Mia stripped away her clothing and then rinsed it in the water, freshening it with her small bar of soap and wringing it out. She hung her dress and undergarments to dry on tree branches and then plunged into the water, gasping from the shock of the cold, but still relieved —the last time she had freshened up was quite a while ago, in the creek near the fur trapper's cabin. Mia took deep breaths and closed her eyes as she dipped her head back into the frigid water, letting it wash the sweat and grime away from her skin and hair.

Mia's eyes shot open when something splashed nearby. At the edge of the spring, a woman hunched over, a shroud of bearskin falling around her body. She dipped a tightly woven basket into the water. As the woman looked up, her eyes widened at the sight of Mia. In a hurry, she picked up her basket and left.

Mia finished washing and stepped out of the water, finding a large, flat rock to stretch out and dry her body in the sun. Like the climate of southern Dakoris, the air of the Loriar forests was dry and crisp. It did not take long for Mia's skin and clothes to be ready to go. As Mia put her underthings and her dress back on, it occurred to her how much weight she had lost after days on foot and her recent mediocre luck with hunting, probably an unhealthy amount. Her ribs showed and the dress hung loosely around her waist. Hopefully, Mia would have the opportunity to rest and eat plenty when she reached Beriniat and collected the inheritance.

As she left the spring, Mia discovered a well-worn footpath through the trees, in the direction where the woman in the bearskin cloak had gone. After following it for some time, Mia stumbled upon a rock with a circular carving bored into it, the god and goddess of olden times. This carving did not look aged and wind-worn like the others she'd found scattered along the way. This was recent art.

The trees parted to reveal a brilliant wildflower-dotted meadow ringed by towering, pointy firs. In the center of the meadow was a surprise. Signs of human life, a cluster of wooden cabins. People dressed in bear and wolf furs roamed from cabin to cabin, arms loaded with baskets.

Mia picked her way down the hill, her bag weighing heavily on her body. A light-haired woman of the Enyo race and a dark-haired man turned, noticing her. They both held the hands of a small brown-haired girl. A baby was wrapped on a wooden board attached to the man's back.

"Hello?" Mia called.

"Hello there," said the woman. "Where do you come from?"

"You're not with the military, are you?" the man asked, narrowing his eyes. His voice had a lilt a bit different from the other Loriar natives she had encountered so far.

"No, I'm not," Mia assured them. "I'm from a long way away. I'm on a journey to Beriniat to collect an inheritance for some orphaned boys. It's a long story."

"You look tired," the woman commented. "Why not stay a spell? You don't have any companions with you, do you?"

"I'm traveling alone. What is this place?"

"How good are you at keeping a secret?" the man asked.

"I have had plenty of practice at that."

"Good. Because our little village is one of them. Come along."

The couple led Mia to a large, round, central building with a domed ceiling. A hole in the top of the ceiling let out aromatic smoke from a fire in the middle. Suspended above the fire, sweet-scented soups bubbled in iron pots.

The couple served Mia a cup of nutty-flavored soup. It was delicious, and in her hungry state she slurped it up fast. All around Mia, people ate and chattered merrily.

The sun was beginning to set. An impromptu celebration of some sort began as people went outside to dance and twirl in each other's arms. A band played, blowing into lively-sounding pipes and beating on resonant leather and wood drums. At random, Mia was tossed from one dancer only to spin into another stranger's arms. Ale was passed around. The music got louder, as did the laughter. Mia danced and twirled until she got dizzy, nearly forgetting about her problems. She drank ale until she was tipsy. In some corners, villagers shed their animal skins, and other garments as well.

Late that night, as the partying continued outside, the man who had been one of the first to speak with Mia led her to a small thatched-roof hut and rolled out some bearskin bedding and straw for her to lie down on. He put his two young children to sleep on small pallets.

"You sure I can stay here?" Mia wanted to confirm.

"Of course. You seem a friendly soul."

"Who are you people? What is this place?"

"I am Moto, and you met my wife, Rhee. We practice the old ways."

"The old ways?"

"We live the way our people have lived for centuries. Living with and loving each other instead of slavery and torture. Worshiping the God and Goddess of All."

"Goddess?" Mia remembered the history professor in Parem City mentioning the goddess who was now banned from the public religion in Loriar, with severe penalties involved.

"What's a god without a goddess? She has been against the law of the land for so long now, most people have forgotten about her. The kings think we're more civilized without her."

"What I've been seeing in this part of the world doesn't exactly look civilized to me." Mia's first thought was the sins of Mr. Totlok. "Men who hate women. Men who starve their slaves."

"After enough generations, and enough priests telling them that nonsense, they think it's just the way the world works. With fear and time, folks can make other folks think anything is normal."

"Yeah, I suppose."

"To worship the Goddess and live by the old ways is punishable by death. Something to think about before you tell anyone about our little settlement."

"I won't tell anyone. That's really too bad. You people just seem so happy. Happier than anyone else I've been running into lately."

"We plan to keep it that way."

"Do you mind if I stay for a while? I do have to get to Beriniat; I've got important tasks there."

"Do you know the way to Beriniat?"

"Sort of. I do have a map, but I'm not certain."

"It's east of here, and a pretty big city. You can't miss it."

"Thank you. I need to get there soon. But I've been through quite an ordeal, and I'm just exhausted."

"You may stay as long as you like. You may find that you'll want to live here the rest of your life. A lot of the folks here wandered in from elsewhere. My friend is from Beriniat and my wife escaped slavery in the mines. And long as you're friendly and don't tell outsiders, we won't object."

"Where is your wife?" Mia asked.

"She's with her lover right now."

Mia reeled at this information, and just how casually the man stated it, before recalling another thing the history professor had told her. Before an angry king dramatically changed the laws of Loriar, it was commonplace for the people to share spouses and lovers.

"And you're not jealous?" Mia asked.

"No, I'm not jealous," Moto told her with a little laugh and a shake of his head.

"I have never had a sweetheart before, but I probably would be going wild with jealousy. It might be different if I were raised here. I wish that everything hadn't changed in this country."

"Me, too."

Tucking themselves into their pallets, they went to sleep, except for the baby, who cried. His mother came back and fed him. Far off in the distance, wolves howled, prowling on the hunt. Mia ached on the inside, wanting to run among them on a chase, the cool moonlit breeze rushing through her fur. But she would not change in the presence of these people, not wanting to scare them, not wanting them to hunt and skin her.

The days that followed were peaceful ones. The people of this nameless little village loved to burst out into food, drink, and parties with or without apparent reason, at any time of the day or night. Joyous, upbeat music was an almost constant background noise. Nearly every family brewed their own ale in wooden barrels. Mia tried to imagine an entire northern country where people lived happy and carefree, in the days before gold mines and hatred of women dominated the public consciousness.

According to the villagers, theirs wasn't the only holdout of the old ways. Other, similar settlements could be found here and there, if you knew where to look.

A small temple contained a colorfully decorated, flower-dotted altar devoted to the God and Goddess of All. The god was muscular and wore only a loincloth, while the goddess had large, hanging breasts and a protruding pregnant belly. An old man explained to Mia that the goddess was the mother of the human race, hence her rounded proportions. A hand-carved, painted wooden arch, representing the ring around the earth, framed the entire display.

Mia helped out by collecting fruit from the small crops and gathering water in the nearby spring, where she also redid her black hair dye job in secrecy. For fun, Mia also braided her hair into coils and stuck freshly picked pink and purple wildflowers into the black tresses. Mia liked this place. It was tempting to just stay and live out the rest of her life here. But Tak and Mendy's boys, now on their own for months with probably no idea that both of their parents were dead, and Mrs. Totlok, freed from her husband's iron fist but now scared and on her own, remained on Mia's mind.

But for now, Mia just needed a break. She needed to drink, dance, listen to the upbeat music, be merry, twirl, and forget. Life hadn't been this slow and enjoyable since the days at Danli's farm. Now, it felt like a million years since that painful and confusing time when Danli had sent Mia away and set this whole trip in motion.

∞∞∞

One bright and sunny day, Mia was sent out with a basket to gather berries. She had to travel on foot for quite a long distance, since most of the edible bushes near town had been picked clean.

Mia's ears perked up at the mumble of male voices off in the distance. Tracking the source of the unintelligible words, Mia crept slowly on silent feet, careful to not let a single twig snap. When she got close enough to make out the words, she hid behind a thick red tree trunk to eavesdrop. In between the men's words were the snorts and whinnies of horses.

"This is so dreadfully dull, being told to roam around out in the middle of nowhere," one voice complained. "I don't think we're going to find anything out here. All we've found is a couple of lunatic fur trappers."

"At least we have some nice pelts to sell. I'm glad we knew just the right way to intimidate that wizened old trapper into giving 'em up. 'Course, it'd be nice if we found the girl. Just think how handsomely we'd be paid."

"Remember, they told us to stop focusing so much on the girl? I don't know what that was all about. I don't think she is even real."

Mia quickly peeked out from behind the tree trunk. Several yards away was a camp site with canvas tents. Three soldiers sat around a smoldering pit of extinguished coals, chewing on food. Their black horses, tethered to pines nearby, restlessly tossed their heads.

"Well, boys, s'pose we should break down this camp and head on?"

"Certainly. I'm anxious to start making our way back to town. I'm tired of being out in the sticks."

Mia hated to imagine what trouble could happen if these military men found the hidden, illegal village. She turned and ran, quick like a fox, with no berries in hand. By the time she stumbled into the meadow, she was gasping for air.

"You have to leave now!" Mia began to warn villagers, stopping the band just as a long-haired older man was raising his hand to beat on the drum. "There are soldiers camped out in the woods nearby!"

Eyes widened immediately. The bearded village elders began to call out, with serious urgency in their voices. "Everyone to the sanctuary! Now!"

The townspeople began to gather up their children, babies, and sacks of essential clothes and items. Within minutes, they were on the run, Mia swept up in the middle of the stampeding herd. They ran through the trees, Mia not knowing where they were going, until they located a crack in the earth underneath a rocky cliff face. They climbed down a precarious, slick path, rocks and pebbles tumbling down the sandy trail into darkness, and lowered themselves into a moderately sized cave. An elder covered the entrance with messy, natural-looking bundles of straw, leaving cracks open for ventilation.

When candles were lit and eyes adjusted, Mia could tell

that this was not the first time this round cave had been inhabited, with a cold fire ring in the middle and a few blankets scattered around. It looked like human hands had dug and enlarged the cave over the years.

Later that night, despite the cold and dark, the group decided against starting a fire in case the smoke coming from the entrance gave them away. Instead, they all snuggled up close for warmth and ate fruit and jerky for dinner. In the group's collective unease, they did not talk much. They drank the bottles of ale that some had brought with them in their packs to soothe their nerves and help them sleep.

Moto, the man who had allowed Mia to stay with his family, crouched next to her and spoke in a hushed tone. "We have been lucky so far when we've had to hide here. But if they find us, all of our heads will roll."

"I certainly hope that it doesn't happen."

"Our happiness is bought at the risk that we're all one drop of the axe away from being with the God and the Goddess. But never fear. The afterlife is a happy one."

"I hope you don't end up in the afterlife anytime soon. And I am afraid that I really must leave for Beriniat soon."

"You may want to leave in the morning. Hurry. Don't let them see you."

"I will. And I will keep all of you in my prayers."

Mia barely slept that night, waiting for soldiers to bust into the cave and round them all up. The ground was rocky and uneven beneath her thin bedding. In the morning, Mia packed her bags, wished all of the villagers well, took the advice, and left discreetly. As soon as she climbed out of the cave, they plugged the entrance with more straw. Already, Mia missed the village terribly.

The days got cooler as summer began to transition into autumn.

Moving in isolation through the forest, Mia experimented again with changing form. When she transformed into a wolf, her clothing and bag of supplies vanished into some alternate space, returning when she transitioned back into her human body. Traveling in this form, especially at night, made things easier and more efficient. The coating of fur kept Mia quite warm. The longer the nights stretched on, the less Mia wanted to assume her clumsier, slower, less agile-footed human form. Instead of fixing fires and camp sites, she slept curled nose to tail in dens during the day and hunted by night.

Mia and the nearby wild wolves located each other by sounds, scent trails, and even thoughts. In the unspoken way of wolves, the animals sent information straight to Mia's head. After she established her benevolence, staying meek, they began to help her even though they sensed that she was not quite like the rest of them. From their signals, Mia gained knowledge of which residences to give a wide berth, which farmers were looking out for canines to kill.

Civilization cropped up—more and more towns, more and more roads. As the wild wolves now communicated wordlessly to Mia, these were signs of the capital city drawing near. There were still thick forests in between the highways and towns, and when faced with the expanses of trees, Mia stayed in her wolf form and hoped that she would not find herself on the business end of a farmer's bolt or arrow.

One evening just before sundown, covertly dashing through the trees near a major road, Mia caught a faint whiff of a scent familiar enough to make her belly clench and her head swim with flashbacks. In her human form, Mia could not have noticed this smell unless she inhaled it up close. But her wolf nose was much more sensitive. And she could not mistake it.

It was the smell of Danli, the shepherdess who had allowed Mia to live with her for years. But that wasn't all. Danli's smell interwove with the scent of Cady, Danli's niece and Mia's onetime best friend. Mia even remembered how Danli's horses smelled. And they'd brought those same horses with them, their hooves treading upon this very road.

They had come all the way here to eastern Loriar.

Why?

Were there important buyers in this area for their goods? For them to travel all this way, there would have to be a very handsome sum of money involved. Mia never knew Danli to stray far from her home unless she had to. And Mia did not remember anyone interested enough in Danli's wool, or the rugs or yarn made from it, for transactions over this long of a distance. Only a select few producers, the best and wealthiest ones in all of Dakoris who offered the prettiest rugs, enjoyed the kind of reputation that would stretch all the way to the Beriniat area. And such a reputation took not only many years but all the right social connections to build up, connections that Danli, with her reclusive nature, did not have.

The other, more likely possibility was that they were looking for Mia herself.

Mia pursued the fresher and fresher trail in the dimmer evening light, staying hidden in the trees whenever she could. Were Danli and Cady searching for Tak and Mendy? Had they found out that the couple were dead? Were they looking for the inheritance, maybe even wanting it for themselves? Had they even decided to team up with the soldiers who'd been chasing after Mia?

Mia resented Danli for kicking her out, even if she understood that fear drove her to it. Since that fateful day, Mia had pushed most thoughts of Danli out of her mind; it hurt a bit to think of her, of the feelings of rejection. At this point, Mia was not too inclined to trust Danli again. And if, for whatever reason, Danli and Cady were chasing Mia all the way to Beriniat, the thought made her skin prickle. Something was wrong with this picture. She now trusted both of them even less.

The scent trail brought Mia to an inn tucked away in the trees behind a large wooden gate decorated with strung-up cow skulls. Still in wolf form, slinking around unseen in the shadows and staying as quiet as she could on her paws, Mia spotted both

Danli and Cady through a downstairs window, talking with each other as they got ready for bed. The window was open a crack. With her keen canine ears, Mia listened in.

"This place is so strange, Aunt Danli," Cady exclaimed, sitting in the bed in her nightgown and pulling a comb through her long, gleaming blond hair.

"I know, Cady. Loriar is rather unsettling. And I know Thom is still on your mind."

"I'm trying not to think about how he's broken my heart."

"A real fiancé doesn't break up with you as soon as you go on a trip."

"I think he believes we aren't coming back."

"Of course we're coming back, m'dear. Don't be silly."

"Ugh, Aunt Danli. This whole trip has been such a pain. You know finding her is going to be like finding a needle in a haystack."

"I know, honey. It's not going to be easy, particularly if she's already made it to the city. But we're so close. We cannot give up now. It's going to be just one more day. I pray we aren't too late."

As the two women braided their hair and snuffed out their candles to go to sleep, Mia turned and loped away. She knew of another pair of faces to look out for with suspicion and avoid when she got into Beriniat. Faces she had once been close to, had once eaten dinner with every night. Whatever they wanted to do with her now, it was best to not find out.

The wolf crested the hill on her lithe legs and then sat atop it, panting. The thick trees had parted, a huge swath of them cut down to make way for the impressive sight that sprawled out before Mia: the capital city of Beriniat, a sea of wooden houses and cobblestone streets amid trees bright with the beginnings of red and golden autumn leaves. Plumes of fragrant smoke rose from the chimneys into the lightly overcast gray sky. Far off, atop a small knoll at the city center, was Mia's ultimate destination: the royal palace, its turrets topped with gilded round bulbs.

Mia's exhaustion and stress from these difficult past months turned to delight. Hopefully this had all been worth it. But after getting the inheritance and seeing Mrs. Totlok's father, Mia planned on going straight back. She'd already seen enough of the world, at least for now. The world was more dangerous than she had anticipated. It had killed her traveling companions and her horses, and had nearly killed her.

The wolf rose up in height until it turned back into a young woman. The last time she had found a spring not too long ago, Mia had washed her clothes and re-dyed her hair black, so she was ready to be seen in public.

Mia braided her jet-black hair. Heart beating faster with anticipation, she walked down the softly sloping, rocky hill, down to where the houses on the outskirts of Beriniat begin. Trying to keep her hopes up that the future held positive things, Mia set her sights on the palace. What exactly she would do when she reached the huge building, she didn't know; but hopefully a palace worker could point her in the direction of the inheritance. After that, she would go to see Mrs. Totlok's father at the temple to inform him that his daughter was widowed and needed help. Of course, she would have to leave out her own role in Mr. Totlok's death. Whenever guilt stabbed Mia over killing Mr. Totlok, she reminded herself of just what a brutal man he was. And she'd had to defend her own life.

Mia grew anxious to reach the palace. Her only hope was to make it back to Dakoris alive and exist there in peace, with no more strange men looking for her. Mia reached into her bag and patted the clay pendant of Mendy's necklace.

"I wish you were here to see this," Mia said. "I finally made it. I hope you're not still mad at me, wherever your spirit has gone. I wish both you and Tak were here."

The streets got busier with merchants as Mia walked

deeper into Beriniat. She continued her long stroll to the palace.

To be continued...

* * *

Acknowledgement

I owe thanks to my husband, Randall, for his tireless help while this project was years in the making, reading my manuscripts after each revision and helping me with the finer details of the fantasy genre. I would also like to thank my other beta readers, Robert Petretti and Jenny Holm, for their valuable feedback.